ELIZA
And The
Edenton Tea Party
In 1774

Vivian Barbee Coxe
Robert Barbee Coxe
Illustrations by Vivian Barbee Coxe

Cover: A bronze teapot is mounted atop a Revolutionary War cannon in Edenton, NC, to commemorate the Edenton Tea Party.

Manufactured in the United States of America.

ISBN: 978-1-7375893-3-4

First Printing

Published By: Silphium Design LLC

In Memory Of

Elizabeth Green,

our ancestor,

a signer of the

Tea Party Resolution

- VBC and RBC

Variations in the spelling of places occur due to the historical sources used.

Table of Contents

Prologue: An Overview of the American Revolution

On July 4, 1776, the Continental Congress adopted the Declaration of Independence. This document declared the thirteen American colonies independent of Great Britain. The colonists still had to win a war for their independence.

Officially, the first shots of the American Revolution were fired at Lexington and Concord, Massachusetts, on April 19, 1775. For awhile, the war continued to rage, mostly in the Northern colonies. Then Savannah, Georgia, fell to the British in December 1778, followed by the capture of Charleston, South Carolina, May 1780. Next, British General Charles Cornwallis concentrated on North Carolina, and his ultimate goal, Virginia.

Fortunately, the French sent an army and fleet to help the Americans. After six and a half long years, the end of the American Revolution began with the British surrender at Yorktown, Virginia, on Oct. 19, 1781.

Introduction

On October 25, 1774, fifty-one women from five counties met in Edenton, North Carolina, to participate in an event called the Edenton Tea Party. It was one of the earliest known instances of female political activity in the American colonies. They were the wives, daughters and sisters of important governmental leaders and private citizens.

In this novel, Eliza, a courageous young wife, is happily married to Captain Nate. Although fictional, Eliza is representative of those women who took a stand against the British that October in 1774.

Edenton was a coastal town with a population of over five hundred in 1774. It was the capital of the colony from 1722 to 1743. Commerce thrived, culture flourished, and sailing ships regularly visited this major port by the Albemarle Sound.

Map of Edenton in 1774

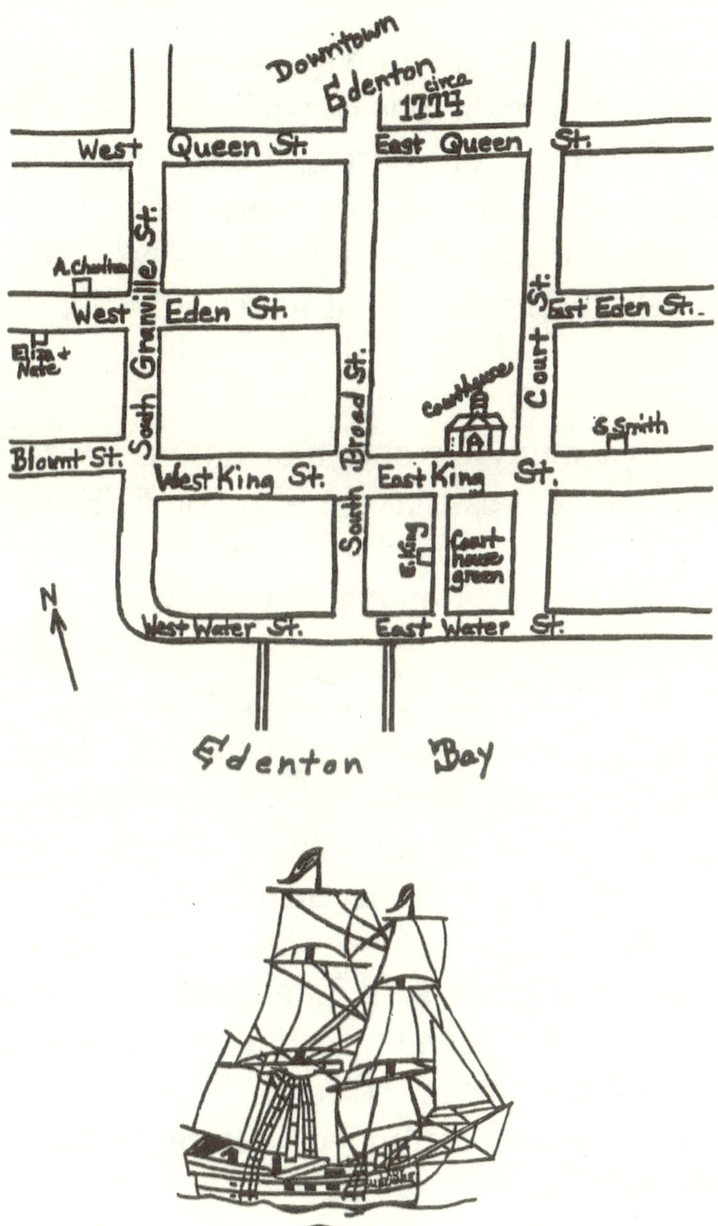

Chapter 1 - The Dressmaker's Shop

Eliza and Captain Nate live on West Eden Street in the prosperous coastal town of Edenton, North Carolina. They are a young couple that will be celebrating their first anniversary soon. The winds of war with England are brewing, however, and it's a time of uncertainty for everyone.

On a sunny October morning in 1774, Eliza walked to the dressmaker's shop on E. King Street in Edenton. She was picking up a new gown and hat for a special party that week.

As Eliza made her way past the tall, longleaf pines and stately houses on W. Eden Street, she waved to Hannah, her next door neighbor. Hannah was hurrying to the market with a large basket on her arm.

At the corner of W. Eden and S. Granville, Eliza stopped to let a horse-drawn carriage clatter down the road of packed sand. Then she crossed S. Granville, and continued walking another block on W. Eden.

Suddenly, Eliza was startled when a brown mouse scurried by her feet. A large, gray tabby cat was chasing the rodent into an alley. The incident reminded Eliza that the European immigrants had introduced cats to the colonies.

Eliza turned right on S. Broad. The main commercial district of Edenton was located on this wide street. Walking on S. Broad toward Edenton Bay, Eliza noticed a few merchants were opening their shops for the day's business.

Nearby, a man secured the reins of his brown horse to the hitching post outside the shoemaker's shop. Above the shop door, a large wooden sign displayed a picture of a black boot below the word, "Shoemaker." Since some people could not read at that time, the shops had signs with both pictures and words.

In the distance, Eliza heard the cries of gulls on Edenton Bay. She spotted her husband's tall ship, the "Lady Albemarle," anchored by a pier at the waterfront. Captain Nate and his crew had arrived the day before from Charleston, South Carolina. They were unloading supplies for Edenton's merchants. Shipments of cloth, salt, sugar, rum, molasses, wine, and medicine were on board the sailing vessel.

Carefully crossing the busy intersection of King and S. Broad, Eliza headed left on E. King. Just as she passed the handsome red brick courthouse, the wind threatened to send her wide-brimmed straw hat sailing across the courthouse green. She pulled her blue shawl closer, and held onto her hat and long, blue flowered skirts.

Eliza's destination was the second house past the courthouse. This charming cottage belonged to Sarah Smith, the dressmaker.

Upon entering the quaint shop, Eliza was greeted by Sarah.

"Good morning, Eliza. Please have a seat in the parlor while I finish fitting a dress. You might enjoy looking at the new rolls of cloth on the shelves and these dolls dressed in the latest styles. I'll be with you in about twenty minutes," Sarah finished.

"Thank you, Sarah."

Eliza admired Sarah, a young widow who supported a ten-year-old son on her income from sewing. Sarah was known as far away as Williamsburg, Virginia, for her skill with a needle and thread.

About fifteen minutes later, Eliza's friend, Mary, came into the parlor from the fitting room. Mary was carrying her new dress in a pretty cloth bag.

"Eliza!" Mary exclaimed. "I'm so glad I've run into you. Sarah just finished my gown for the tea party at Elizabeth King's house this week. Penelope Barker said you were invited. I heard Penelope has invited quite a few out-of-town guests. What are you wearing for the big event?"

"Hello, Mary. Sarah designed a new gown and matching hat for me. They're in blue taffeta trimmed with pink ribbon and lace. The gown has a low-necked bodice, and a ruffled petticoat and overskirt," Eliza replied.

"I can't wait to see your dress at the party," Mary said, as she waved good-bye to Eliza and left the shop.

Sarah returned to the parlor and said, "I've made several dresses for the tea party but yours is my favorite, Eliza."

Showing Eliza the blue gown, Sarah commented, "See how fashionable it is. The fitted bodice has ruffled sleeves."

"It's lovely, Sarah."

"I've combined the European style with my own design. Why don't you try it on? I'd like to see how it looks."

The dress fit Eliza beautifully, yet it seemed to need one more touch. Therefore, Sarah sewed a pink velvet bow on the lacy neckline. It added the perfect detail, and matched the hat. Feeling pleased, she gently packed everything in a special cloth bag and handed it to Eliza.

"I really like the dress and hat," Eliza said. She counted out twenty pounds in British currency from her reticule and gave it to Sarah.

"Thank you very much, Eliza. Enjoy the party!"

The sweet smell of baking bread filled the air after Eliza left Sarah's shop. She decided to stop at the bakery nearby and buy a Sally Lunn ring loaf. Nate was especially fond of this bread. He would enjoy it with the oyster supper that evening. With this thought in mind, Eliza returned home on West Eden. The happily married couple lived in a neat two-story frame house with a wide front porch.

Eliza spent the afternoon working contentedly in the herb garden beside the kitchen. After harvesting several herbs, she tied them in bunches and hung them upside down in the kitchen to dry. The herbs would be used for cooking, medicine, and potpourri.

Chapter 2 - Supper Conversation

Around nine o'clock that night, Eliza and Nate had a relaxing supper at the dining table by the fireplace. Eliza served fried oysters with a garnish of parsley, stewed apples, thick slices of the Sally Lunn bread with butter and strawberry preserves, cheese, and wine. While dining by candlelight near the warm fire in the hearth, they shared the day's happenings.

"Nate, it was good to see the "Lady Albemarle" anchored by a pier at the waterfront. I was on my way to the dressmaker's shop this morning when I saw your ship. I'm wearing the blue gown and hat made by Sarah to the tea party at Elizabeth King's house," Eliza said.

"I'm sure you will be captivating, Eliza. Blue is my favorite color on you. It accents your lovely blue eyes, dearest. By the way, I had dinner at Horniblow's Tavern this afternoon. There was some talk about the tea party. Are you aware that Penelope Barker may be planning some other activities besides drinking tea and socializing?" Nate asked.

“I’m not sure I understand what you mean, Nate.”

“Well, from what I have heard on my business trips, a lot of colonists are unhappy about the British taxes, particularly on East India tea. Much of the conversation at Horniblow’s centered around this topic. Don’t be surprised if Penelope asks the ladies at the tea party to make a commitment of some sort to the cause.”

After Nate sipped more wine, he continued, “Remember, Eliza, that Penelope’s husband, Thomas, is our colony’s agent in London. Also, your dear father is a delegate in the North Carolina Provincial Congress. He told us that East India tea and British manufactured goods were banned by the First Provincial Congress when it met recently,” Nate finished.

“Mary saw me this morning at Sarah’s. She mentioned Penelope had invited a large number of guests who live outside Edenton. It does appear this may not be a typical afternoon tea, Nate.”

He replied, “These oysters are delicious, my sweet. I hate to leave town again so soon, dear, but I must take a shipment of food and supplies on the “Lady Albemarle” up to a port near Boston, Massachusetts. The port of Boston has been closed by the British since June 1st this year, and North Carolina is helping by sending provisions to the people there. The British are punishing Boston because of the colonists who dumped 342 chests of East India tea in the Boston harbor last December. As you know, the event was called the Boston Tea Party, and it was a protest against the Tea Act. The crew and I will be departing in two days. In the meantime, I have a gift for you. I hope you like it, dear.”

He handed Eliza a fancy blue velvet pouch, tied with blue satin ribbons.

“Oh Nate, what a surprise!” she cried.

Eliza untied the blue ribbon on the pouch, and reached inside the cloth bag. She pulled out a dainty, silver heart-shaped locket on a short length of sturdy black velvet ribbon.

“It’s absolutely beautiful!” Eliza exclaimed.

Nate fastened the special locket around her neck.

He said, "I thought you might want to wear the necklace to the tea party. I have a bigger plan in mind, however. After I return from my trip to Massachusetts, I'm taking the two of us on a nice long sail to the West Indies on the "Lady Albemarle." You can wear the locket and the new blue gown for me as we celebrate our first anniversary in the islands."

"Nate, you always have such splendid ideas. I miss you so much when you are out at sea. It will be wonderful to be with you on the "Lady Albemarle" again like we were on our honeymoon."

Visions of the West Indies voyage floated through Eliza's and Nate's thoughts that night as they drifted off to sleep.

Chapter 3 - Tea Party Resolution

Before putting out to sea again, Nate hired a horse-drawn carriage for Eliza's transportation to the afternoon tea party. Attired in her fancy blue dress and hat, she enjoyed the pleasant ride to Elizabeth King's house opposite the courthouse green. Many carriages were already lining the street when she arrived. At least I'm not too early, she thought.

Penelope Barker greeted each guest at the front gate.

"Eliza," Penelope said, "I'm so glad you came. You look lovely. Please join the other ladies in the garden."

"Thank you, Penelope. I've looked forward to the party," Eliza replied.

By 4 o'clock, the garden was filled with guests in their best dresses and hats. They visited among the clusters of purple and white asters, and the goldenrod blooming in the garden.

Penelope welcomed the assembled group of fifty-one women in her usual cheerful manner.

"Good afternoon. It's wonderful to see everyone here. Isn't this a beautiful day for a tea party?"

Then Penelope's face became business-like as she continued.

"As most of you are aware, the First Provincial Congress met at New Bern on Aug 25th. At that meeting, the Provincial Deputies of North Carolina resolved not to drink any more tea from Britain after September 1st nor to import British products except medicine after Jan 1, 1775, because of the taxes on them."

Penelope paused for a moment, and then continued.

"Our leaders felt that taxation without representation in Britain's Parliament is unacceptable. To show support for the resolves passed by our delegates, I have prepared a resolution. It reflects our willingness not to use tea imported through Great Britain, and to stop purchasing manufactured goods from the British. Keep in mind, please, that these goods are still being sold in our colony. I will now open the floor for discussion on this matter," Penelope finished.

"Tea is almost a universal drink of the colonies, Penelope. If we give up tea, what will we drink in place of it?" asked a woman named Anne.

"We'll do the same as some of us have already been doing since the passage of the Tea Act. We can drink tea made from dried raspberry, mint, sassafras, or yaupon leaves instead of the British tea. Other beverage options are milk, cider, coffee, or chocolate," Penelope explained.

"Penelope," asked Margaret, "is this resolution to include only us, or everyone in our family?"

"We are showing our patriotism as individuals and also by setting an example for our families to follow. Hopefully, our influence will spread beyond Edenton," said Penelope.

Lydia asked, "Is our tea party in any way similar to the Boston Tea Party?"

Penelope smiled. "There is a major difference between our tea party and the Boston Tea Party on the night of Dec 16, 1773. The Sons of Liberty in Boston disguised themselves as Mohawk Indians before they dumped 342 chests of East India tea into the Boston Harbor."

Penelope continued with emphasis. "We, on the other hand, will not hide our identities. I challenge each of you today, Oct. 25, 1774, to bravely and proudly sign your name to this resolution. Let me read it to you."

"As we cannot be indifferent on any occasion that appears nearly to affect the peace and happiness of our country, and as it has been thought necessary, for the public good, to enter into several particular resolves by a meeting of Members deputed from the whole Province, it is a duty which we owe, not only to our near and dear connections who have concurred in them but to ourselves who are essentially interested in their welfare, to do every thing as far as lies in our power to testify our sincere adherence to the same, and we do therefore accordingly subscribe this paper, as a witness of our fixed intention and solemn determination to do so."

"I'm ready to sign the resolution now," said Abigail, one of Eliza's neighbors.

"Me, too," said a woman from the far side of the garden.

Penelope replied, "Thank you. That's wonderful. The resolution is written on this scroll which I will place on a table in the parlor. An ink stand with ink and a quill pen will be provided. Please form a line by the table to sign your name. Tea brewed from dried raspberry leaves and also assorted tea cakes will be served in the dining room. We will make a toast after everyone has had an opportunity to sign the resolution."

Standing in line to sign the resolution, Eliza said, "This is really exciting, Mary. I wonder if anyone will remember the Edenton Tea Party in years to come?"

“That is a good possibility,” said Mary, “especially since we have a written document. By the way, your blue dress and hat are very becoming, Eliza.”

“Thank you for the compliment, Mary,” said Eliza.

About thirty minutes later, Penelope said,” Ladies, I’m very happy to announce that all fifty-one of us signed the resolution and have now formed an Association. This is a great way for us to show our patriotism.

“We’ll make our toast now,” Penelope announced.

Holding their teacups high, the ladies repeated, “To the pursuit of liberty from English rule!”

“Here, here,” the woman chorused.

Today, the Edenton Tea Party is considered one of the first political activities by women in the American colonies.

These were the proud, courageous ladies who signed the Resolution:

Abigail Charlton
F. Johnstone
Margaret Cathcart
Anne Johnstone
Margaret Pearson
Penelope Dawson
Jean Blair
Grace Clayton
Mary Bonner
Lydia Bonner
Sarah Howe
Lydia Bennett
Marion Wells
Anne Anderson
Sarah Mathews
Anne Haughton
Elizabeth Vail
Mary Creacy
Mary Creacy
Ruth Benbury
Sarah Howcott
Sarah Hoskins
Mary Littledle
Sarah Valentine
Frances Hall
Mary Jones
Anne Hall
Rebecca Bondfield
Sarah Littlejohn
Penelope Barker
Elizabeth P. Ormond
M. Payne
Elizabeth Johnston
Elizabeth Beasly
Mary Blount
Elizabeth Creacy
Elizabeth Patterson
Jane Wellwood
Mary Woolard
Sarah Beasley
Susannah Vail
Elizabeth Vail
Elizabeth Cricket
Elizabeth Green
Mary Ramsey
Anne Horniblow
Mary Hunter
Tresia Cunningham
Elizabeth Roberts
Elizabeth Roberts
Elizabeth Roberts

Chapter 4 - Reactions

Eliza and Nate returned home to Edenton from their West Indies trip in Feb. of 1775. While visiting various islands, they heard differing accounts of Britain's reaction to the resolution signed by the women at the Edenton Tea Party. Most reports indicated that the female participants openly defied the British authority. Also, by signing their names in support of the resolves passed by the North Carolina Provincial Congress, they had in effect, joined forces with the men, in a protest against the British taxes.

The "Morning Chronicle and London Advertiser" printed an article listing the signers of the resolution. It was published on January 16, 1775, and included a political cartoon of the tea party. In the satiric drawing, the faces of some prominent British politicians replaced those of the female signers, suggesting that the women were acting like men. This caused quite an uproar in the British upper circles.

It is worth noting that in the eighteenth century, a woman's name in the news was considered socially unacceptable, except for birth, marriage, and death notices. Needless to say, Parliament was keeping a close watch on the Tea Party Signers.

One day in early spring, Nate shared information with Eliza concerning the tea party. He heard the news from some reliable sources at Horniblow's Tavern.

Nate said, "I'm sure you remember James Iredell, the noted Edenton lawyer. He recently received a letter from his brother, Arthur, who lives in London. Arthur reportedly asked James if there was a female Congress in Edenton, and said that he hoped not, for the Englishmen are already afraid of the male Congress. Arthur even claimed Edenton as one of the places in America that has plenty of "female artillery."

Nate looked at Eliza and commented, "What a compliment that was to the political power of the tea party participants, my dear."

"Yes," Eliza replied, "women have been heard."

Nate hugged Eliza then, and said, "I'm so proud of you and your courage, Eliza."

She kissed him gently on the cheek and responded, "Thank you, Nate. Your opinion means a lot to me."

Other colonial women were inspired by the brave women in Edenton. In March 1775, Janet Schaw recorded that some ladies in Wilmington, North Carolina, burned their tea "in solemn procession but they had delayed, however, till the sacrifice was not very considerable as I do not think anyone offered above a quarter of a pound."

In early October of 1775, Eliza and Nate became the proud parents of Caroline Elizabeth. They began a family tradition by designating Oct. 25th as a special time to honor the courageous women of the Edenton Tea Party in 1774.

Chapter 5 - A Toast to 1776

Lively carols echoed throughout Eliza and Captain Nate's parlor on New Year's Eve. Their neighbors happily joined Nate and Eliza's father, James Anderson, in singing, "Deck the Halls," "Ding Dong! Merrily on High," "I Saw Three Ships," and "Wassail Song." Eliza played the accompaniment on the harpsichord.

"That was enjoyable," Eliza said. "Let's adjourn to the hall for wassail and holiday sweets."

The merry friends followed Eliza through the passage to the festive hall. It was a sight to behold. Each windowsill was decorated with sprigs of holly, pine, and dried hydrangea. Similar greens adorned the mantel that held Nate's model ship, the family heirloom clock, and a pair of candlesticks. Remnants of the Yule log and branches of aromatic rosemary burned brightly in the fireplace.

Encircled by oranges, apples, and greenery, the wassail bowl graced the the center of the dining table. Four beeswax candles in shiny silver candlesticks flanked the large bowl of hot, spiced cider. Also on the table were assorted platters heaped with sliced fruitcake, gingerbread, pecan and mincemeat tarts, jumbals, candied orange peel, and spiced nuts.

Eliza served each guest a cup of fragrant wassail laced with Nate's rum.

Accepting a drink, Abigail Charlton said, "Your gold brocade gown is lovely, Eliza. The decorations are attractive too."

"Thank you, Abigail. My sister, Anne, came from Baltimore to help me. She even brought us oranges from the Bahama Islands. Anne will join us soon. She is upstairs with Caroline."

"Isn't Caroline almost three months old, Eliza?" asked Hannah Edwards. "I hope Caroline manages to stay well. Robert said a number of his Edenton patients have terrible coughs," Hannah stated.

"Caroline was born in early October. Because of the cold I seldom take her outside, but you're kind to be concerned, Hannah," replied Eliza.

Standing near the warm fireplace, Dr. Robert Edwards asked Nate, "In your travels, does it appear that there are more Patriots than Loyalists?"

"Hmm," Nate mused. "It is hard to say." Wearing his long brown hair tied at the back with a black ribbon, Nate was fashionably dressed in a white silk ruffled shirt, gold brocade waistcoat, dark blue wool breeches and matching coat, white silk stockings, and buckled shoes. He leaned back on his heels, and paused for a long smoke on his pipe. "My feeling is that most of those I talk to at major ports are in favor of separating from England. Some are not. Only time will tell," he finished.

Eliza's father, James Anderson, gently tapped a spoon on his cup. "May I have your attention, please?" he asked everyone. Raising his cup, he said, "I'd like to propose a toast. To all of us – good health, happiness, prosperity, and courage for what lies ahead in 1776."

"Here, here," everyone replied as they clinked their cups together.

"James, I hear you are a delegate from Tyrrell County. Would you kindly share information from the Third Provincial Congress held this past August in Hillsboro?" asked Jasper Charlton, a lawyer.

"A lot of territory was covered at that meeting," James began. He stopped momentarily to drink the wassail. Then James said, "There was an urgent need to establish a temporary government since royal governor Josiah Martin fled to a British warship in July. We decided that the new government would bind us to all the acts and resolutions passed by both the Provincial Congress and the Continental Congress. The committees of safety are now the basis for local government. We also created a Provincial Council to coordinate military affairs. Two regiments of five hundred men each were authorized for the Continental Line, and real currency was issued to provide funds for the army. As you know, North Carolina was earlier divided into the military districts of Edenton, New Bern, Wilmington, Halifax, Hillsboro, and Salisbury. Each of those six districts is now required to raise a regiment of six hundred minutemen to be ready, at a minute's notice," he finished.

"I understand our own Samuel Johnston is a leader in the Provincial Congress," Robert stated.

"That's correct," replied James. "Samuel is effective as the presiding officer. He was elected president after John Harvey died in May. We're also fortunate to have Joseph Hewes of Edenton continue to serve us in the Continental Congress."

"I frequently do business with Joseph's mercantile and shipping firm in town," Nate added.

"James, do you think independence from England will happen in 1776?" Jasper further inquired.

“I’ll be happy to comment after I get some more of Eliza’s outstanding wassail,” replied James.

Eliza refilled her father’s cup. Then she offered the beverage to the other guests.

After taking a few sips of his drink, James said, “Several events have made the sentiment toward independence stronger than ever. You may have heard about Patrick Henry’s stirring speech. He spoke on March 23rd at the second Virginia Convention at St. John’s Church in Richmond. His unforgettable words were, “I know not what course others may take, but as far as me, give me liberty or give me death!” On April 19th the flames of rebellion were fanned in Massachusetts. The British tried to seize military stores belonging to the Patriots. As a result, war officially began at Lexington and Concord.”

At this point, James stopped to revive the flames in the fireplace. He added another log and squeezed the bellows to breathe air on the embers.

Returning his attention to Jasper, James continued. “Closer to home, the “Mecklenburg

Declaration of Independence" was approved on May 20th, followed by the Mecklenburg Resolves" on May 31st. The resolves are one of the most daring documents to denounce British authority," James finished.

Nate said, "There has been considerable talk at Horniblow's Tavern about the Edenton minutemen. It was rumored that someone even wrote to Joseph Hewes in Philadelphia to request a drum and a red flag inscribed with "Liberty or Death."

"I'm not at all surprised," James responded. "The situation with the Highland Scots in this colony does not look good right now. It will be interesting to see whether the Scots join forces with Governor Martin and the Loyalists, or with the Patriots. Governor Martin's rating with the Patriots is at an all-time low."

Robert asked, "Have any of you heard of the connection between Bermuda and George Washington, our Commander in Chief of the Continental Army?"

Nate volunteered. "According to scuttlebutt, there was an unusual deal. Earlier this year, General Washington wrote to the Bermudians to request gunpowder they were known to have. At the time, Bermuda was desperate for food because of the conflict between England and the American colonies. The brave men who stole one hundred Kegs of gunpowder from the British powder magazine in Bermuda were never caught. As a reward for this goodwill, the Continental Congress authorized the shipment of a year's supply of food to Bermuda. Ironically, we've been fighting the British with their own gunpowder!"

"That's justice for you," Robert laughed.

All eyes turned as Anne entered the hall. Anne was wearing an elegant green taffeta gown that accented her long, curly red hair. She walked over to James and hugged him. "Father, your granddaughter takes after you," Anne said. "Caroline doesn't want to miss anything, especially music. Thank goodness, I finally got her to sleep," Anne teased.

James responded, “We’re sorry you were unable to join us earlier, dear. Gentlemen, may I present Anne Carter, my youngest daughter from Baltimore? Anne, meet Dr. Robert Edwards, and Jasper Charlton,” he said with pride.

“The pleasure is mine,” Robert said.

“I’m delighted to meet you,” added Jasper.

“Thank you,” replied Anne.

Smiling at Anne, Robert said. “I trust you are having a pleasant stay in Edenton. Our town is smaller than Baltimore but charming in its own special way.”

“To be honest, Edenton is one of the prettiest towns I’ve seen,” Anne remarked. “I’m impressed by the lovely architecture here, and the bay is beautiful. It has been a marvelous experience visiting with my new niece, and of course, Eliza, Nate and Father. Perhaps my husband can join me on my next visit,” Anne continued.

Nate said, "Anne and I will sail for Baltimore in two days. James is also sailing with us to his home across the Albemarle Sound. The crew is on board the "Lady Albemarle" making preparations. We're carrying naval stores from this area up to Anne's husband, David Carter, who is a shipbuilder. He's an old friend of mine. In fact, I introduced Anne to David. The sea is definitely in our family's blood," Nate chuckled.

Eliza walked over to Anne and asked, "Would you like some refreshments, Anne?"

"That sounds wonderful, Eliza."

Anne graciously accepted a cup of wassail and fruitcake from Eliza. The sisters talked several minutes by the table, and then joined the other ladies sitting at the windows. Dressed in colorful gowns, the group was a cheerful sight.

"Hannah and Abigail, I'd like you to meet my sister, Anne Carter," Eliza proudly announced.

"Hello, Anne," said Abigail.

"I've heard so many good things about you," Hannah stated.

"I'm glad to meet both of you. By the way, Abigail, Eliza told me that you attended the famous Tea Party last year with her," said Anne.

Abigail smiled. "That party was such a historic event for women. The British were angry because we protested the tea tax. Our names were even published in the London newspaper," she said.

The four ladies discussed the joys and challenges of rearing children. They also shared recipes and talked about the latest fashions.

Eliza excused herself from the women. She picked up a special basket on the sideboard. It was filled with fragrant rosemary from her herb garden. She gave each guest a sprig of rosemary for remembrance.

Noting the time on the clock, Nate spoke in his authoritative captain's voice. "Your attention, please. I have a special surprise for you. Grab your cloaks and meet me outside on the front porch in three minutes."

Right at midnight, two loud BOOMS were heard from the harbor as blanks were fired from a cannon aboard the "Lady Albemarle." The bells of St. Paul's Church rang in the distance, too.

"Happy New Year!" Nate proclaimed joyously to his family and friends gathered on the porch. "Happy New Year!" everyone responded to Nate and to each other too.

Chapter 6 - Baltimore Trip

The Fells Point waterfront near Baltimore, Maryland, bustled with activity on a chilly, windy morning in late Feb. 1776. Workers at the Carter Shipyard were cutting, shaping, and fastening white oak timbers to form the huge framework of a sailing ship. It took approximately twenty-three different craftsmen to build each one. Just recently, Captain Nate had placed an order for a new schooner designed by his brother-in-law, David Carter.

Across the cobblestones between the shipyard and several plain warehouses, fishmongers hawked the day's catch. Down at the docks crews called out orders while unloading their varied cargoes from distant ports.

Among those vessels preparing to put out in the Patapsco River was the "Lady Albemarle" of Edenton, North Carolina. David Carter stood on the dock to bid farewell to Nate.

"Fair winds!" David shouted.

From the helm of the "Lady Albemarle," Nate waved to David. Carefully, Nate eased his seventy-foot ship away from the dock and into deeper water. The buildings of Baltimore soon disappeared from view.

Within an hour, the 2-masted brig was almost full-rigged, and sailing fast and majestically on the Chesapeake Bay toward the Atlantic Ocean. Having cleared with the customs official, the "Lady Albemarle" was carrying iron, sails, saddles, coffee, wool blankets, soap, flour, salt, sugar, rum, and wine. Also on board were several copies of Common Sense by Thomas Paine. This recently published pamphlet about independence was spreading like a wildfire across the American colonies.

A few days later off the coast of Virginia, Nate gave orders to his crew of eight. "We're going to tie up to the privateer, "Eastward," he said. "I'm going to board her and purchase four kegs of gunpowder from their captain. Benjamin and Crispus, would you help transfer those kegs to our ship? Label "flour" on each one in recognizable writing, and stash all of them among the real kegs of flour in the hold."

“Aye, Captain,” replied Benjamin and Crispus in unison. The two brothers were freemen and had crewed with Nate for almost a year.

Nate was pleased the purchase at sea went smoothly. He would now be able to donate some needed supplies to the Edenton minute- men. Scanning the skies, however, he was not happy to see the dark gray clouds quickly gathering ahead.

Sudden winds from the northeast sent waves of green water crashing over the deck of the “Lady Albemarle.” Her bow dipped deeper into each wave trough, and rose back up, shaking to and fro. Sheets of rain hammered relentlessly across her pitching, rolling, wooden deck. It was becoming increasingly difficult for the helmsman to steer into the waves.

“All hands on deck! Prepare to heave-to, lower the storm sail, and secure the other sails to the spars,” Nate yelled to his crew over the wind.

For two days, the northeaster tossed the “Lady Albemarle” about like a toy boat. The ship’s crew worked non-stop to keep her afloat on the angry sea. By the third day, weary but safe, they finally got back on course toward Edenton.

At the entrance to the Roanoke Inlet on the North Carolina coast, Nate sighted a large flock of gulls, several dolphins, and two warships. He had a sinking feeling that trouble was brewing. Rather than taking his usual route, he sailed farther south to Ocracoke Inlet. The crew commented about Blackbeard, the pirate, who was killed near Ocracoke Island in 1718.

Local pilots known as loyal Patriots helped the "Lady Albemarle" to navigate the dangerous shoals of the inlet. Then the ship sailed on the Pamlico Sound to the Albemarle Sound and to Edenton.

Crew spirits soared when the lookout spotted the cupola atop the Corbin House by Edenton Bay.

While entering the harbor, the ship moved slowly to the "Dram Tree." This old cypress was known to bring good luck to those mariners who followed the tradition. Nate leaned over the rail and poured some rum into the special keg near the tree's middle. It was the custom for all captains leaving port to drink a dram of the rum for safe passage.

Shortly after the ship docked, Nate hurried home to Eliza. He swept her into his arms, and kissed her. Sensing that she was worried about something, he gently asked, "What's wrong, dear?"

"Oh, Nate, I'm so glad you are home. Have you heard about the Battle of Moore's Creek Bridge?"

"No, dearest, I haven't. Please tell me about it."

"We got a letter today from my cousin, Sampson. He was wounded in battle. I'll read the letter to you while you unpack your things."

"March 3, 1776

Dear Eliza and Nate,

How are you? I broke my left arm on Feb 27th at Moore's Creek Bridge. This place is located outside Wilmington. Even though I was among the forty or so wounded, I count myself fortunate. At least thirty from our side were killed. The Patriots reportedly lost one soldier and had fifty casualties.

Around dawn, under the acting command of Colonel David McLeod, I was carrying my broadsword and playing the bagpipe. I fell on the greased girders of the bridge, and into the chilly creek. The Patriots had removed the planks. Somehow, I managed to crawl out of the creek. I hid in the underbrush and escaped capture. The battle lasted about three minutes! It is hard to believe the Patriots defeated our much larger force of Loyalists, who were mostly Scottish Highlanders. The outcome might have been different if General MacDonald had not become ill before battle. We had marched all the way from Cross Creek.

Regardless of what happens in the coming weeks, please know that I send my best to you and your family.

Your cousin,

Sampson Stewart

P.S. It's a good thing I write with my right hand!"

"I'm glad Sampson survived," Nate said. "The war is growing closer. Maybe that is why I saw a couple of warships around Roanoke Inlet on the trip home. Eliza, are you feeling well? How is Caroline? I've really missed both of you."

"I've been sick almost every day since you left for Baltimore, Nate. Dr. Edwards told me that I'm expecting again, and the baby is due in August. Hannah has helped me by taking care of Caroline when I have been quite weak. Caroline is fine. She is taking her nap. Oh, I almost forgot. Father sent us a letter too. He is going to Halifax in April to attend the Fourth Provincial Congress. I'll brew a pot of mint tea to go with some biscuits and jam, and you can share about your visit with Anne and David."

“Eliza, dear, I’m so sorry you haven’t been feeling well, but I’m happy to hear about our good news. Speaking of your father, I bought a special pamphlet for him. I’ll mail it tomorrow. I also have gifts for you and Caroline. Hopefully, I can stay closer to home for awhile,” Nate said tenderly, as he hugged Eliza again.

Chapter 7 - Halifax Resolves

The morning sky was partly cloudy on Thursday, the 4th of April. It was a cool day and signs of spring appeared throughout the small town of Halifax, by the Roanoke River. New leaves clothed many trees. Birds sang and early wildflowers were blooming in a rainbow of color.

Halifax was a trading center and the seat of government for Halifax County. The townspeople welcomed the fifty-eight delegates, who had just arrived for the opening of the Fourth Provincial Congress. More would arrive shortly. Rooms were already becoming harder to find at the local taverns, inns, and private homes.

Royal power in the colony of North Carolina essentially ended with the Patriot victory at the Battle of Moore's Creek Bridge. Now, more than ever, the representatives were ready for change.

Before taking a congressional seat at the courthouse, each delegate was required to subscribe to the Association Test. This agreement was related to a series of resolutions adopted by the Continental Congress in Oct. 1774. It included the right of the American people to "life, liberty, and property."

Allen Jones of Northampton County stood and faced the assembled group of delegates. Smiling, he said, "The Fourth Provincial Congress is now called to order. It gives me pleasure to propose that Samuel Johnston of Chowan County continue to serve as president. All those in favor, please signify by saying "aye."

"Aye," chorused all of the delegates.

"It is unanimous. Mr. Johnston remains president," Allen Jones announced.

Rising, Samuel Johnston said, "Thank you. It is an honor to lead such a distinguished group of citizens. Our work is cut out for us through mid-May. Please plan to meet every day except Sunday. I'm confident that by working together we can make a major difference for independence," he finished.

President Johnston appointed a secretary and two door keepers. It was also resolved that the freeholders of Halifax would be asked to meet the next day and elect a delegate to replace Allen Jones's brother, Willie Jones, who had been called out of town. The first day's business was completed.

Later that afternoon, James Anderson was eating a hearty dinner at the popular Liberty Tree Tavern near the courthouse. As he casually looked around, he noticed another delegate approaching him.

"Hello, My name is John Hinton. May I join you?" asked John, extending his hand to James.

'It would be my pleasure, John. By the way, I'm James Anderson."

Placing his tricorne next to James's hat on an adjacent chair, John said, "Please continue with your meal. I think I'll order the same."

“You won’t be disappointed. The fricassee with rice is superb, and the sweet potatoes have just the right amount of cinnamon,” James added.

A short time later while savoring the tender chicken seasoned with spices and herbs, John asked, “Where is your home, James?”

“I’m from Tyrrell County. I’ve attended all four Provincial Congress sessions. How about you?” James inquired, sipping more wine.

“I represented Wake County at the Second Provincial Congress in Newbern and also the Third Provincial Congress in Hillsboro. Perhaps you’ve met my son-in-law, Joel Lane, of Wake County?”

“I haven’t had the pleasure of meeting him, but I recall his name from an earlier Congress. Have you found a room yet? I’m staying at Mrs. Miller’s house on Dobbs Street. Mrs. Miller told me she had two beds left this morning,” James offered.

“I’d be very obliged if you could help me find a place to stay,” John replied. “I just arrived in Halifax this morning, and I'm still trying to get my bearings after fighting at the Battle of Moore's Creek Bridge."

"You were at that battle, John? I'd like to hear about it. Allow me to order some gingerbread and coffee for us."

Over dessert, John reflected, "I'm rather surprised we beat the Loyalists. Their side numbered roughly sixteen hundred men while ours was only about a thousand Patriots. Originally, the Highland Scots were going to march from Cross Creek to Wilmington. At that point they planned to join forces with Sir Henry Clinton's Boston troops, and a British army of invasion which would make a landing on the Cape Fear River. Both General Cornwallis's troops and a fleet under Sir Peter Parker were expected. Luckily for us, our victory at Moore's Creek Bridge stopped the Loyalists from realizing their scheme. I understand Clinton didn't arrive at the Cape Fear River until March, and Cornwallis and Sir Peter Parker have yet to appear."

James laughed, “So much for great plans,” he said. “I’ve heard some of the men who were captured at Moore’s Creek are housed in the jail across from the courthouse,” he finished.

John added, “Their fate will be decided by Congress during this session.”

“Tell me about your militia. How big was it, and did you have much ammunition?” James questioned.

The young attentive serving girl poured more coffee.

“After raising two companies, I had about 157 men in the Wake militia. Our company was under my son, Captain James Hinton. Our group joined units from other counties and the minutemen. I purchased 30 dozen gun-flints and 25 ¼ pounds of lead. Higher officers have told me that ammunition continues to be in short supply for us. We’d be in serious trouble if the British had invaded the southern colonies,” John said.

“My son-in-law, Nate, is a sea captain from Edenton. Whenever possible, he brings ammunition and supplies to the colony. Recently, Nate brought me a copy of Common Sense. Have you read it? I strongly recommend Thomas Paine’s pamphlet to anyone who values independence. You may borrow my copy if you’d like,” James urged.

“Thanks, I’ll return it to you as soon as I can. Let’s pay for our meals, however, as I still need to find some lodging,” John said.

On James’s recommendation, Mrs. Miller rented her last bed to John. Taking advantage of the leisure time, James took a nap; meanwhile, John returned to the courthouse to pick up his bags. A thin, young man in disheveled clothes approached John. “Sir,” the stranger said, “I’m looking for work to pay for my supper. Could you please help me?” he pleaded.

“I’ll let you carry my two bags to Dobbs Street for five shillings,” John replied, handing the bags to the other man.

“Bless you, kind gentleman. I haven’t eaten for two days. Please allow me to introduce myself. I’m Hamilton McLean, and I was captured at the Battle of Moore’s Creek Bridge.” Balancing the two bags, Hamilton tried to match John’s walking speed.

“Do you have a family?” John asked.

“My dear wife is due to have our first baby any day now. She has no idea where I am or even if I’m alive. Somehow, I’ve got to get a letter to her but I don’t have money for postage,” Hamilton said, his voice slightly breaking.

“Don’t you worry. Meet me outside the courthouse tomorrow afternoon at three o’clock with your letter, and I’ll see that it is mailed,” John reassured him.

“Thank you,” Hamilton whispered. Gratefully, he accepted the money from John after leaving the bags in front of Mrs. Miller’s house.

Around nine o’clock, John and James walked to the Liberty Tree Tavern for a light supper. Some other delegates joined them for a spirited discussion about the difficult road to independence.

Later, in his room at Mrs. Miller's house, James wrote to Eliza. He dipped his quill several times in the inkwell before completing the letter. Feeling very tired but hopeful that Eliza would send news, he blew out the flickering candle and went to sleep.

During the first week, the members of Congress listened intently while letters were read aloud from the three North Carolina delegates to the Continental Congress in Philadelphia. William Hooper, Joseph Hewes, and John Penn wanted to know how the North Carolina Provincial Congress viewed the deteriorating relations between the colonies and Great Britain.

Committee assignments were made over the next several days and more delegates arrived and subscribed to the Test. At least eight different committees met at a variety of places in and around town. A typical day might include breakfast, Congress from 9:00 AM to 3:00 PM, dinner, committee meetings from 4:00 PM to

9:00 PM, and finally supper and free time. Sunday was the only day of rest from this rigorous schedule.

John Hinton's committee was organized on April 5th. The twelve members were asked to find out and report to Congress on the amount of ammunition currently in the colony.

On Monday, April 8th, James Anderson was assigned to Cornelius Harnett's committee of seven. These delegates had the task of studying the usurpations and acts of violence committed or attempted by the King and Parliament of Britain against America. The committee was charged with finding solutions for better defending the colony of North Carolina.

By Friday morning, April 12th, dogwood in magnificent white bloom greeted the town. Cornelius Harnett felt optimistic as he walked to the courthouse. His committee had worked hard to develop some resolutions for Congress to adopt.

"Good morning," Samuel Johnston addressed the eighty-three delegates. Various items on the agenda were covered. Then Mr. Johnston turned to Mr. Harnett and asked, “Is your committee ready to present its report?”

“Aye, Mr. President.”

“You may proceed.”

Cornelius Harnett of Wilmington rose slowly from his seat. He looked out at the sea of faces and began speaking in a serious tone. “Gentlemen, what I am about to say may shock you. Our committee has carefully reviewed the facts and options. We strongly feel that Congress needs to act soon.”

For almost half an hour, Mr. Harnett cited numerous instances of usurpations and violences committed or attempted by the King and Parliament of Britain against America. After taking a few minutes to confer with his committee, Mr. Harnett continued with the recommendation.

“Resolved,” he said with fervor, “That the delegates for this colony in the Continental Congress be empowered to concur with the delegates of the other Colonies in declaring independency, and forming foreign alliances, reserving to this Colony the sole and exclusive right of forming a Constitution and laws for this Colony, and of appointing delegates from time to time (under the direction of a general representation thereof), to meet the delegates of the other Colonies for such purposes as shall be hereafter pointed out."

Several gasps were made aloud.

"It is time for North Carolina to be heard!" James Anderson exclaimed.

"Aye. We must surely take a stand," another delegate shouted in agreement.

Soon the delegates were talking excitedly in groups of two and three.

President Johnston called the Congress back to order. The bold resolution was discussed vigorously by the whole group before everyone adjourned for an early dinner. A vote would be taken later that day.

That evening, Mr. Johnston told the delegates, "We are going to vote now. All those in favor of the resolution from Mr. Harnett's committee, say aye."

"Aye," resounded throughout the room.

"Those opposed, say nay," said Mr. Johnston.

There was a moment of silence.

Mr. Johnston proudly announced, "It is done. The resolution is unanimously passed. Hopefully, our document will create patriotic waves throughout the American colonies. Please accept my sincere thanks. Good night."

Many delegates celebrated the momentous event at the Liberty Tree Tavern. The lively crowd made toasts to liberty and freedom till the wee hours of the morning.

Over the weekend horse races were held at a nearby track. James Anderson commented to John Hinton, "This scenery reminds me of my childhood home in Virginia. We had close to a thousand acres and bred race horses on the side."

Congress stayed busy throughout the next month. During this time an unsuccessful attempt was made to create a constitution for North Carolina. Instructions and orders were drawn up for recruiting officers. John Hinton was among those promoted. He was appointed Colonel for Wake County on April 22nd. Funds were also approved for military provisions. The Council of Safety was formed on May 11th to replace the Provincial Council.

"Good afternoon. I'm looking for my father-in-law, James Anderson," Captain Nate inquired of Mrs. Miller on May 13th.

"Mr. Anderson probably won't return from Congress until this evening. I'll tell him you were here," Mrs. Miller replied.

A few hours later, James was pleasantly surprised to spot Nate at the Liberty Tree Tavern. The two men exchanged news over supper.

James said, “Nate, your letter arrived yesterday. I’m concerned about Eliza, too. Please tell me how she is.”

“She continues to have problems with this pregnancy.” Nate confided.

“I don’t want to alarm you,” replied James, “but my dear Margaret died shortly after giving birth to Anne. Eliza was only two years old at the time.”

“I’m really sorry about Margaret. Eliza told me that her mother died many years ago but I didn’t know the cause. Here is how you can help, James. I’m sure a surprise visit from you will lift Eliza’s spirits. That’s why I invited you to go back to Edenton with me,” Nate added.

James said, “That sounds like a good plan. We need to stop at my place, however, so I can pick up a special gift for Eliza.”

“We can easily sail to your house before continuing to Edenton,” Nate replied.

“This is changing the subject, James, but have you heard anything about the British raids along the lower Cape Fear River?”

“The latest news I have from Congress is that the British are heading for Charleston, South Carolina,” James shared.

May 14th was the last day of the Fourth Provincial Congress. A standing ovation was given to Samuel Johnston for serving as president. It was announced that the Fifth Provincial Congress would meet in Halifax on Nov. 10th unless advised earlier by the Council of Safety. Mr. Johnston praised the delegates for the important work they accomplished. Finally, the Congress adjourned, and the men bade their farewells.

John Hinton stood at the Halifax waterfront by the Roanoke River and waved to James Anderson. Captain Nate and James were departing the pier on the “Lady Albemarle.”

Chapter 8 - A Special Visit

Several days later Eliza answered the front door. Two men stood on the porch.

"Hello, Eliza," James said, smiling.

"Father!" she exclaimed, hugging him.

"What a wonderful surprise!"

Nate stepped forward. He whispered in her ear, "I didn't go to Virginia after all."

Laughing, she replied, "You two never cease to amaze me. Well, let's get out of the wind. Please, come in. We can catch up on the news over tea."

The next afternoon Hannah stopped by Eliza's house. James and Nate were out running errands.

Hannah asked, "Eliza, could you please come over and give me your opinion? I can't decide which shoes and hat to wear with my new gown."

"I'll come if I can bring Caroline," Eliza said.

"That will be fine," answered Hannah.

The two women walked next door with Caroline in Eliza's arms. At the Edwards's house, Hannah led Eliza and Caroline through the passage to the hall. Everything was quiet until suddenly…

"SURPRISE! Happy Birthday, Eliza," chorused Hannah, Robert, James, and Nate. Even baby Caroline smiled.

With a look of astonishment, Eliza commented, "I was so thrilled to see Father and Nate yesterday that I even forgot today is my birthday. How thoughtful of everyone to remember me."

For the party, Hannah had filled the charming room with vases of fragrant pink roses from her garden. She offered each guest a slice of homemade rum cake. Eliza poured the "liberty tea" while Nate held Caroline.

Back at Eliza's and Nate's house, there was another surprise for Eliza. After supper James handed her a small wooden box. Carefully, she unpacked the protective cotton inside and discovered a pretty white teapot with a raised floral design. A matching sugar bowl and creamer completed the set.

"Father, your gift is beautiful, Thank you!"

He explained, "This set is very unique. It belonged to your mother, who received it from her mother. Your mother loved you very much, Eliza. I hope you will continue the family tradition, and pass the set on to Caroline."

"That's a wonderful idea. Thank you again for the perfect gift."

Eliza set the treasured teapot next to Nate's model ship on the mantel. It would be used for special occasions only.

It was soon time for James to return home. Nate was taking James back to Tyrrell County on the "Lady Albemarle."

On the morning of departure, it was sunny and breezy at the waterfront. James stood on land near the pier, while Nate kissed Eliza and Caroline goodbye. Then Nate proceeded to board the "Lady Albemarle," and completed the last minute preparations. A crew member carried James's bags on board the ship.

James hugged Eliza and bent down to kiss Caroline, who was struggling to get out of Eliza's arms.

"Bye, Papa," Caroline cried.

"Bye, bye sweet child," James said soothingly to Caroline. He stroked Caroline's long brown curls. Gently, he told Eliza, "Please take good care of yourself and Caroline, and my grandchild-to-be."

Eliza replied, "This was one of my best birthdays ever. Have a safe trip back home, Father."

Nate signaled to James that it was time to depart. Quickly, James walked up the gangplank and climbed aboard the bobbing ship. He waved to Eliza and Caroline. Soon the vessel was under way on the bay and heading for the rougher waters of the Albemarle Sound.

Eliza was grateful for the carriage Nate had hired that day. The driver had patiently waited after driving Eliza, Nate, James and his bags, and Caroline to the waterfront. Now Eliza and Caroline were riding in the same carriage back home. Eliza enjoyed the relaxing ride past the large, fine houses on W. King, S. Granville, and finally W. Eden. The horse's rhythmical hoofbeats lulled Caroline to sleep on her lap. Exhausted but happy to be home, Eliza placed Caroline on the bed and lay down beside her for an afternoon of rest.

Chapter 9 - Declaration of Independence

During the sail to Tyrrell County, Nate asked James about the Fourth Provincial Congress. In particular, Nate wanted to hear about the document that directed the North Carolina delegates in Philadelphia to vote for independence from Great Britain.

After returning to Edenton, Nate shared the information with some of the leaders of St. Paul's Church. They decided to write a declaration to affirm their allegiance to the King, but also to express their desire "to maintain and support all and every the Acts, resolutions and regulations of the Continental and Provincial Congress to the utmost of our power and ability." Nate was among those who signed the document on June 19th.

One morning in July while Nate reviewed the cargo list on the "Lady Albemarle," a young man delivered an urgent message. The note requested Nate to report immediately to the Hewes' shipping firm.

It was Market Day in Edenton. Many people were in town to buy special foods and crafts. Exotic merchandise was also available from the ships at anchor.

Nate threaded his way through the noisy crowds along the waterfront and the courthouse green. He passed the courthouse and Horniblow's Tavern, and stopped at the Hewes building on the corner of Broad and E. King Street.

Upon entering the prestigious shop, Nate was approached by a courteous clerk.

"Good morning, Captain Nate," the clerk said. "I have invited James Iredell to meet with you. He will be here in about 10 minutes. Please feel free to sit down."

"Thank you," replied Nate, settling into a comfortable chair by the front window.

James Iredell arrived shortly. A noted lawyer and customs official at the port of Edenton, Mr. Iredell was a familiar figure to Nate. The two men shook hands.

"Hello, Mr. Iredell," said Nate.

"It's good to see you, Captain Nate," answered Mr. Iredell. "Let's move to another spot for privacy."

James Iredell led the way to a small office. He indicated a chair for Nate, and then sat opposite him at a table.

"Well," said Mr. Iredell, "I guess you are curious about the purpose of our meeting. No doubt you've heard about the British attack on Fort Moultrie in Charleston harbor on June 28th. Since the British found out the South is not easy to invade, they are now focusing their attention on the North. I received a letter recently from Joseph Hewes in Philadelphia. Joseph said that the Continental Congress is making history. He also reported that the Continental Army has a shortage of ammunition. Joseph wanted me to personally ask you a favor. He wants you to secure as much gunpowder as possible from your contacts that are sympathetic to the Patriot cause. The Hewes firm will reimburse you for all expenses. It will also transport the powder to the army," he finished.

Nate responded, "That's quite a challenge! Please tell Joseph that I'll do my best. The crew and I will sail within the week."

James Iredell stood. Smiling, he said, "Thank you for your help, Godspeed, Nate." The two men shook hands again before Nate left the office.

Before Nate put out to sea a few days later, he arranged for Hannah to check on Eliza. There were still times when Eliza was sick. Caroline required attention, too.

It took about two weeks for Nate to complete his "gunpowder mission." The "Eastward" captain sold Nate his last two kegs of powder. Nate was advised that the "Atlantic Rover" might have some powder to sell.

After weathering a storm on the Atlantic Ocean for several days, Nate located the "Atlantic Rover." She was found off the coast of Virginia one moonlit night. Her captain and crew were in low spirits, and they were more than willing to trade gunpowder for rum. Fortunately, Nate had a plentiful supply of rum. He agreed to trade ten puncheons of rum for five kegs of powder. First, Nate's crew tied up to the other ship and quickly transferred the rum to the vessel. Then they carefully moved the powder to the "Lady Albemarle." Loud, bawdy sea chanteys drifted from the "Atlantic Rover" as the "Lady Albemarle" sailed away on the calm sea.

Back in Edenton, Nate's crew delivered seven kegs of valuable gunpowder to the Hewe's warehouse on the waterfront. A Hewes' official gave each crew member a special pass to be used for dinner and unlimited drinks at Horniblow's Tavern.

An impressive sleek schooner tied up at an Edenton pier on a warm, sunny afternoon in early August. Several people stopped to admire the vessel's dark blue hull. It was decorated with a row of thirteen white stars on both the starboard and port sides of the bow. There was no name on the ship.

Nate stood several minutes near the mystery ship and studied it. Suddenly, he did a double-take when a man and a pretty woman with long, curly red hair appeared on the deck and waved at him.

"Nate!" Anne called. "Please come aboard."

"Anne and David! This is a surprise! I didn't recognize your ship!" Nate cried, leaping up the gangplank.

Nate hugged Anne, and shook hands with David.

"How do you like you new ship, Nate? I wanted to personally deliver her to you. She sails beautifully!" exclaimed David, smiling broadly.

"I can't believe this incredible ship is mine," Nate replied, with genuine enthusiasm. He walked over to the helm and held it while admiring the attractive vessel. "You've done a remarkable job, David. We'll take her out for a sail on the Albemarle tomorrow. Right now, though, I want you to come home with me. Eliza will be thrilled to see you," he finished.

The three friends piled into a hired carriage, along with an assortment of bags, and rode to W. Eden. On the way, David commented, "I have a lot to tell you, Nate."

Anne, sitting next to David, said, "I'm excited about visiting with Eliza and little Caroline again."

Nate chuckled, "Caroline has grown so much," he said. "She is ten months old now, and loves to explore her surroundings."

Anne responded, "She must be a handful for Eliza. It's a good thing I plan to stay several months. I'll be able to help Eliza before and after the baby arrives."

"Anne, you are an angel," remarked Nate. "It's so nice to have you and David here," he added.

At the house, Nate and David got absorbed in a discussion about ships.

Taking turns tending Caroline, Eliza and Anne prepared a simple dinner of leftover sliced ham, beaten biscuits, green beans, fresh berries, and tea or wine. They fed Caroline and tucked her into a small bed for a nap.

Later, seated around the dining table, the four adults happily shared the meal after Nate gave the blessing.

David buttered a biscuit and sampled it. "Mmm, this is delicious," he said to Eliza.

"Thank you," Eliza replied. "You might even try some ham on the biscuit," she suggested.

Then David announced, "I have some big news. Several weeks ago a friendly fellow from Philadelphia stopped by my shipyard for repairs. His name was Gideon, and he told me about the recent events in the Continental Congress. A resolution stating the colonies should be free and independent states was passed on July 2nd. This document is called the Declaration of Independence. Thomas Jefferson of Virginia helped to draft it. After some recommended changes were made, the Congress officially approved the Declaration on July 4th. Delegates from every colony are being asked to sign.

Nate asked, “But that’s committing treason, isn’t it?”

“Yes,” David answered in a serious tone. “Benjamin Franklin reportedly said, “Now we must all hang together or assuredly we shall hang separately.” David sipped some wine and continued. “We will have to fight hard for our independence. It will not come easily. There is a story circulating around that John Hancock, president of the Congress, was the first to sign the Declaration. He used a bold signature so King George III could see it without his glasses.”

“Well, it sounds like John Hancock is an exceptionally brave person,” Nate added, smiling.

David said, “The Declaration was read publicly for the first time in Philadelphia on July 8th, Gideon was among the large crowd cheering outside the Pennsylvania State House. A great bell was rung after the momentous reading.”

Nate responded, "It's an exciting, but dangerous time to be a Patriot. North Carolina declared independence on April 12th. We encouraged other colonies to do the same."

Eliza stated, "We can be proud that Father was a delegate to the Fourth Provincial Congress. He helped to pass the important document called the Halifax Resolves that was about our independence."

Anne agreed, "That's an excellent point, Eliza. By the way, have you heard about Nate's new ship? I think he is still in shock from seeing us this afternoon," Anne said, laughing.

"Nate mentioned that you and David sailed in a new schooner. Please tell me about it, David," Eliza requested.

"This vessel is designed to be a swift merchant ship. It is one of my finest schooners. The overall length is sixty feet, and the dark blue hull has thirteen white stars on the bow. We're going sailing tomorrow if the weather is nice," David explained.

“The ship sounds beautiful,” Eliza said. She continued, “I’d love to sail with you, David, but I’m not feeling very energetic these days.”

Anne offered, “I’ll stay here with Eliza and Caroline while you and Nate play with the ship.”

Chapter 10 - New Beginnings

The next week David sailed back to Baltimore in the "Lady Albemarle." He planned to refit the ship and return it to Nate by the Christmas holidays. Anne would be staying with Eliza and Nate in the meantime.

Eliza woke up one morning several days later and called for Anne. "Please go and get Hannah. I'm not feeling well," Eliza said.

Anne replied, "Maybe the baby is on the way. I'll come back as quickly as I can."

When Anne returned about fifteen minutes later, Eliza was struggling to catch her breath.

Hannah arrived in less than ten minutes. "Eliza, I've contacted Robert. He is coming over as soon as possible. Anne and I will look after Caroline. Please try to relax as much as you can. We will be here with you," Hannah said.

Eliza appeared to drift in and our of consciousness. She asked for Nate. Anne said,

"Nate is away on business. He is returning home this evening."

The labor pains were so sharp at times that Eliza cried out. Then she went back to sleep on her bed.

Dr. Robert Edwards came and examined Eliza. He realized she needed assistance from him. Hannah would help, too.

After two more hours of hard labor, Eliza gave birth.

"You have a beautiful daughter with red hair," Robert said to Eliza. Totally exhausted, Eliza just nodded, and fell back on her pillow.

After Hannah cleaned up the crying newborn, she gently dressed her in a diaper cloth and a long white cotton gown. Then Hannah held the baby so Eliza could rest awhile.

Robert asked Anne to get some lavender and mint tea for Eliza.

The delightful fragrance of the lavender helped revive Eliza. With Anne's support, Eliza managed to sit up and sip the soothing tea.

Hannah placed the hungry baby in Eliza's arms. Eliza nursed her daughter. Soon, both mother and baby fell asleep. Anne sat nearby and kept a close watch on them.

Nate arrived home about 8 o'clock that night.

"How is Eliza?" Nate whispered to Anne. The candlelight flickered and cast shadows on the walls of the bedroom.

"Congratulations, Nate," said Anne, in a lowered voice. "You have another pretty daughter. Eliza and the baby are resting. Robert Edwards got here just in time. He said the baby was not in the normal position. Eliza had a difficult delivery. Caroline is with Hannah and Robert."

"Thank you, Anne. I don't know how Eliza would have managed without your help," Nate said.

Nate went over to Eliza and lightly kissed her on the cheek.

Eliza opened her eyes and said in a weak voice, “Take a peek at our daughter.”

“She’s a beauty, just like her mother,” Nate said tenderly, as he gazed lovingly at their baby with red hair.

Early the next morning, Nate went outside and found a beautiful red rose in the garden. He presented the sweetly scented rose, along with tea and a biscuit, to Eliza when she awoke.

“This rose is a small token of my love for you and our new daughter,” Nate announced. “Have you thought of a name for our precious little one?”

“I’ve been thinking of a few possibilities, Nate. The one I like best is Liberty. What name do you prefer?”

“Liberty is a fine name, my dear Eliza, and Liberty Rose is perfect,” he replied.

Faintly smiling, Eliza said, "I love our choice."

By September, Eliza had regained much of her strength. She wrote a letter to her father to tell him about his new granddaughter. Baby Libby appeared to be healthy. When visitors came, Caroline pointed proudly and said, "See the baby."

Nate spent several weeks in town after Libby was born. One bright autumn day Nate decided to name his magnificent schooner after his youngest daughter. The "Liberty Rose" would be a sister ship to the "Lady Albemarle."

Over ale at Horniblow's Tavern, Nate talked with a fellow captain about the upcoming October 15th election. About 169 delegates would be elected to represent thirty-two counties and nine towns at the Fifth Provincial Congress at Halifax.

Nate asked, "Do you know the basic issues between the conservatives and radicals?"

"Aye," the friend said. "Samuel Johnston and James Iredell are conservatives and favor a strong executive. Willie Jones of Halifax is a leader of the radicals. His group wants a weak executive and a strong legislature. I've heard that some of the candidates have exchanged heated words," he finished.

"It appears this will be an interesting campaign to follow," Nate commented.

By October Nate was back at sea on his new ship, the "Liberty Rose," and picking up supplies from privateers for the army. On the way home, Nate sailed to his father-in-law's estate. He tied up at a nearby pier.

James was thrilled to hear more news about his new granddaughter, and admired the ship named after her. The election results had just been announced. James was re-elected to serve as a delegate for Tyrrell County. He would report to Halifax on November 12th for the opening session of Congress.

Nate arrived home a few days before Eliza's tea to commemorate the famous tea party held two years ago. Anne and Hannah were invited to celebrate the occasion.

On October 25th, Eliza proudly served raspberry tea and tea cakes to her guests seated in the cheerful parlor. Vases of pretty purple and white asters were attractively displayed throughout the room.

"Eliza, I like your lovely white teapot and matching creamer and sugar bowl," Anne said.

"The set belonged to Mother," Eliza explained. Then Eliza, raised her teacup and said, "I'd like for us to make a historic toast – to the pursuit of liberty from English rule."

Anne and Hannah raised their teacups, and said in unison, "Here, here."

Anne suggested, "Let's start a tradition, Eliza. Each year on this date, we can hold a tea. I'll introduce the idea to Baltimore. I think you and the other women were really brave to sign the resolution and send it to England."

Eliza replied, "The tradition actually started last year. Shortly after Caroline was born, I made a toast with Nate. I'm glad you want to join me , Anne. Women in the other colonies should know that the ladies in Edenton were heard."

The cooler days of November meant that winter was approaching. Eliza received a letter from her father. He was in Halifax again and staying at Mrs. Miller's house. His news indicated that Congress might meet until right before Christmas. Among the major items on the agenda was the drafting of a state constitution. The delegates would determine the direction of the first state government.

Eliza answered her father's letter within the week. She invited him to spend the Christmas holidays in Edenton. Nate would meet him in Halifax on December 23rd.

One crisp morning in mid-December, a sailor was in the shrouds of the schooner, the "Liberty Rose." Suddenly, he shouted, "A big ship is approaching. The "Lady Albemarle" is sailing beside it."

Nate and his crew crowded around the rail to watch the two vessels moving toward the waterfront. Nate could see that David Carter was at the helm of the "Lady Albemarle." Cheers went up from Nate and his men when the "Lady Albemarle" tied up to its sister ship, the "Liberty Rose." David's 3-masted schooner, the "Baltimore Star," was ninety feet long and required the largest pier in port.

The sailors assembled on the courthouse green. Nate happily announced, "Welcome to Edenton. Let's all adjourn to Horniblow's Tavern. The drinks are on me." Everyone clapped at the good news, and then headed for the tavern on E. King Street.

In another week Nate and David sailed to Halifax. The "Lady Albemarle" seemed almost like a new ship. David had overhauled her and enlarged the living quarters.

James was picked up at the pier on the Roanoke River in Halifax on December 23rd. Heavy rain and winds slowed their progress. That evening Nate anchored in a sheltered cove by the Albemarle Sound.

Down below in the main salon, Nate asked James about the highlights of the Fifth Provincial Congress. James explained, "The state constitution was drafted and adopted, along with the Declaration of Rights, and power shifted from the executive to the legislature. Richard Caswell was appointed the state's first governor. Of particular interest to me, the state constitution provides that "all useful learning shall be duly encouraged and promoted in one or more universities."

Nate commented, "This was an important Congress to attend. Our family is proud of you, James."

The ship's rocking was becoming more noticeable but Nate felt confident that the vessel's anchor would hold adequately. He decided to turn in for the night, and the others soon followed. Waves slapped against the hull of the ship while they slept.

It rained hard most of the next day, too. Sailing across the Albemarle Sound continued to be difficult.

By the time the "Lady Albemarle" docked in Edenton, it was Christmas Day. Church services had already ended. The weather was cold and overcast as Nate, James, and David walked through the streets past the shops and the houses decorated with greenery. They were happy to get home at last.

"Merry Christmas!" the three men shouted, after opening the front door. They hugged and kissed Eliza and Anne, who greeted them in the passage.

The sisters had prepared a big meal. They set the dishes of favorite foods on the elegant table in the hall. Fragrant garlands of pine and rosemary added a festive touch. The Yule log blazed in the fireplace.

James offered the blessing at the special family dinner that afternoon. Then he told his loved ones, "All in all, 1776 has been an exciting year of new beginnings First of all, our family was blessed with another precious baby, who is taking a nap with her sister right now.

Pausing, James continued. "We are fighting for our independence from the British," he continued, "but we are also starting a new nation and a new state. The coming days will offer hope and opportunities for everyone. Then he raised his glass. I propose a toast – to Eliza and Anne for this wonderful feast!" James said.

"Here, here," chorused Nate and David.

Over good conversation, the delicious meal was enjoyed by all.

Chapter 11 - Green Ridge

On a frosty February morning in 1781, Captain Nate stood by his mother's sickbed, and held her cold, frail hand. Holding back tears, the eldest son tenderly said, "I love you, Mother."

"I love you, too," whispered the pale fifty-two year-old woman. She was wearing a long-sleeved white cotton shift. It was tied with ribbons that matched her soft blue eyes. Wisps of reddish-gray hair peeked out of her mobcap.

Moments later, the dear lady suffered another spell of deep coughing. She also had difficulty with breathing.

Nate propped the large feather pillows against the high mahogany headboard, and helped his mother into a sitting position. Then he gently pulled the linen sheet, a blue wool blanket, and the beautiful "Blue Basket" pattern quilt around her thin shoulders. To take the chill out of the air, he also added more wood to the dying embers in the fireplace, that was in his mother's elegant blue bedroom on the second floor.

Nate had sailed his ship, the "Liberty Rose," from his home in Edenton, North Carolina, to his mother's house in Virginia. His mother lived at Green Ridge, a handsome two-story frame house, on a hundred acres overlooking the James River.

Martha, the only daughter, was also staying at Green Ridge. How good it would be to see Martha, and get an update on Mother, Nate thought.

After searching for Martha in several rooms, Nate found her in the cheerful Georgian yellow passage downstairs. He hugged his sister, and asked, "Has a doctor been here?"

Sadly, Martha explained, "Our doctor joined the Continental Army so there has been no medical help available. Even my herbal remedies have failed to improve Mother's condition.

Pausing to compose herself, Martha continued. "I'm really glad you are here, Nate. A neighbor came by last week to check on us. Mr. Burns informed me that traitor Benedict

Arnold anchored at Westover on the 4th of January. A large number of British ships sailed up the James River. There were rumors that Arnold and his troops were on their way to Richmond, our new capital," she finished.

"That's close," Nate replied. "This was a dangerous time to sail, Martha. Your letter arrived in late December, but the British activity off the Carolinas delayed me, as well as some bad storms. I had a close call on the Chesapeake Bay. Fortunately, the fog and cover of darkness made it easier for my ship to pass through the blockade. By the way, have you heard any news from Jesse?" Nate asked.

Martha answered, "His last letter was brief. He indicated that his Virginia militia is under Brigadier General Edward Stevens, and they are desperate for clothes and shoes. Mother asks me about Jesse almost everyday."

Nate commented, "Jesse is her youngest son, so that is understandable. This is changing the subject Martha, but I must go to Williamsburg now to find a doctor for Mother."

Nate opened the front door, and dashed outside.

Quickly grabbing a red wool cloak from the wall peg, Martha fastened the warm garment at her neck. She followed her older brother as far as the stoop. A cool breeze whipped around her long green skirts, and threatened to muss the beautiful long brown curls under her mobcap. As Martha looked toward the river for a glimpse of Nate's schooner, she noticed that only the top of the masts were faintly visible in the fog.

Carefully threading his way past the large oak, beech, and holly trees that were partially hidden in the mist, Nate descended the sloping path at Green Ridge, to the familiar riverbank. He walked across the old pier and landing that his late father had built.

For a few moments, Nate stopped to catch his breath. With pride, he admired the neat row of thirteen stars, one for each colony, that decorated each side of the ship's bow. Soon he was back on board his topsail schooner with the dark blue hull.

The crew of eight assisted Nate with the ship's departure. After weighing anchor, the main staysail was struck. As the vessel got under way again in the James River, a flock of Canada geese, heading west, honked overhead in their V-formation.

Standing watch near Nate, Benjamin said, "I'm sorry your mother is sick, Captain. Don't worry, we'll find a doctor," he added reassuringly.

"Thank you, Benjamin. You have a kind heart," Nate responded from the helm, as he kept his eyes alert to the ship's position in the river. A light rain had started falling, as the fog began to lift.

They were sailing east. Within minutes, the ship was passing Westover, the site where Arnold's troops had recently anchored.

Nodding to the port side, Nate commented to Benjamin, "See that brick manor on the hill? Westover was built by William Byrd II and it has a special tunnel that leads to the river as an escape from the Indians. The Byrd children and I used to play hide-and-seek in the secret passageway."

Nate's thoughts of childhood were interrupted when he noticed the threatening clouds gathering ahead. All of a sudden, the wind changed from a westerly direction to northeasterly. It picked up considerable speed, too, while heavy sheets of rain began to pour down from the dark sky. Tree branches snapped like twigs along the shoreline.

As the ship rocked precariously from the strong winds, the crew struggled to maintain their balance. The men hurriedly secured the sails to the spars and raised the storm sail. Amidst the flurry of activity, a pulley worked loose and crashed on top of Benjamin's head. Blood spurted out of the wound and streamed onto his face and clothes.

Nate and Crispus rushed to help Benjamin, who was sprawled unconscious on the deck. With the utmost care, they managed to move Benjamin to Nate's cabin, where they placed him on the bed.

Crispus applied pressure to Benjamin's wound to slow the bleeding. "I'm glad Benjamin was wearing a hat. The accident might have been worse!' Crispus exclaimed to Nate.

"Even so, the cut is deep and will need stitches," Nate replied. "My original plan was to find a doctor for my mother. Hopefully, this same doctor can tend to Benjamin's injury, too. In the meantime, if Benjamin wakes up, here is some whiskey to kill his pain," Nate finished, handing the bottle of liquor to Crispus.

Relieving the First Mate at the helm, Nate cautiously steered a course toward Jamestown. Floating tree limbs littered the river, which still churned from the high winds of the storm.

Chapter 12 - Dr. Brown

Upon reaching the landing by Jamestown, the crew helped Nate secure the schooner's lines. All were relieved that no British warships were patrolling the area.

Nate quickly disembarked , and raced down the weather-beaten pier. Continuing by foot for almost a quarter-mile, he stopped at a friend's house near the end of the winding dirt road. Perhaps Colin can help me locate a doctor, Nate thought, as he knocked on the door of the neat frame house.

"Good afternoon," Nate said to the attractive young woman who opened the door. "Please allow me to introduce myself." Then he continued, "My name is Nate, and I'm looking for Colin Reed. We were classmates at the College of William and Mary. A member of my ship's crew is badly injured, and he needs medical attention."

"Hello, I'm Susannah Reed. Colin's law office is in Williamsburg. If you hurry, you might find Colin having dinner at the Raleigh Tavern. Perhaps you will find a doctor, too, as there are no doctors in Jamestown. You are welcome to saddle one of our horses. I'm sure Colin will be glad to see you," Susannah finished.

"Thank you for your kindness, Mrs. Reed," Nate replied.

The storm had left debris scattered along the road to the former capital of Virginia. Nate was grateful that Patriot, the horse, managed to gallop without mishap over the treacherous six miles.

It was Market Day in Williamsburg. Nate rode Patriot along the wide Duke of Gloucester Street past the courthouse and Market Square, where vendors were still selling household wares and food to afternoon shoppers.

Horse-drawn carriages rolled by the stylish shops and frame houses as Nate approached the famous Raleigh Tavern. He tied the horse's reins to a hitching post, and stepped inside the popular dining place.

Groups of professional men were seated at dark wooden tables in the public dining room. They appeared to be talking excitedly about the British occupation of the Chesapeake Bay region. Through a veil of smoke from men enjoying their pipes, Nate spotted Colin and another man at a table by the fireplace.

"I can't believe my good fortune!" Nate exclaimed, as he stood by Colin's table. "Colin, your wife said you might be here."

"Nate?" asked Colin. "It has been several years since I last saw you. Please pull up a chair and join us."

Nate and Richard shook hands. Colin said, "This is Richard, my law partner."

Colin explained to Richard, "Nate is a friend from William and Mary."

Nate said, "I have an emergency. One of my ship's crew has a serious injury and I need a doctor."

Nodding his head toward a man who was sitting by a window, Colin said. "Dr. Joseph Brown is excellent. By the way, Nate, you just caught me before I return to the cavalry next week. I'm a captain in Colonel William Washington's Virginia Regiment," Colin finished.

"I'll pray for your safety, Colin. Thanks gentlemen, and please excuse me," Nate replied, before walking over to Dr. Brown.

A few minutes later, Nate and Dr. Brown left the Raleigh Tavern.

"I'll follow you on my horse," Dr. Brown said, as he lashed his medical bag behind the saddle.

"Be sure to watch for fallen tree limbs," Nate cautioned. "We had a bad storm this morning on the James River."

Nate and Dr. Brown rode close together on the rain-drenched road to Jamestown. They stabled the horses in Colin's barn, and then walked to the dock, and boarded Nate's tall ship.

Dr. Brown examined Benjamin, who was still unconscious.

"Because the wound is deep," Dr. Brown said, "I'll have to dilate the opening, and discharge fluids that might cause an abscess to form. I need someone to hold Benjamin's head, in case he should wake up while I'm working."

Nate assisted Dr. Brown, who finished the bleeding into a bowl. Next, Dr. Brown dipped a crooked needle in oil, and stitched Benjamin's long wound, using waxed shoemaker's thread.

"Please keep Benjamin comfortable and quiet, especially if he should regain consciousness in the next few hours," advised Dr. Brown.

Nate turned to Dr. Brown and pleaded, "Could we now please sail to Green Ridge, which is near Westover? My mother is in desperate need of medical care."

"I'll be glad to help, Nate, if you can bring me back to Jamestown tomorrow," Dr. Brown replied.

"That is not a problem," Nate assured him.

The return sail to Green Ridge went smoothly, but Nate's mother had taken a turn for the worse.

Dr. Brown said, "It appears that your mother has fluid build-up in her lungs. That is why she coughs so much. After bleeding her with a lancet, I will use a trocar to draw off the excess fluid. There is a big possibility that she may not survive the procedure since her heart is so weak, but I'll do the best I can to save her."

During the night, Dr. Brown stayed with the patient to check on her progress. In the early hours, however, Dr. Brown called for Nate and Martha to be at their mother's side during the final moments.

As planned, Nate took Dr. Brown to the Jamestown dock the next day. Handing a generous payment to Dr. Brown, Nate said, "I'm deeply grateful for all your efforts to help my mother and Benjamin. God bless you."

The two men shook hands, and departed their separate ways.

On the trip back to Green Ridge, Benjamin miraculously regained consciousness. This was a good sign that helped raise everyone's spirits a bit.

After three days, a simple funeral service was held for Nate's mother. She was buried next to her husband on the Green Ridge estate.

With sadness, Nate and the crew made preparations for the dangerous sail to Edenton.

Chapter 13 - Blockade Escape

“Hold your fire!” Nate yelled from the helm. Under a brisk wind, the British sloop “Falcon” was sailing swiftly toward the schooner “Liberty Rose” on the choppy James River. Eight guns pointed menacingly from the British warship. Billows of smoke erupted from one of the guns that had fired, but missed, Nate’s vessel.

For a fleeting moment, Nate had a sickening fear that he and his crew would be sent to a dreadful British prisoner-of-war ship. Sensing imminent danger, Nate touched the sword on his belt for reassurance. The trusty weapon was a gift from his father, who had fought in the French and Indian War.

Soon the “Falcon” was alongside the “Liberty Rose.” Looking directly at Nate, the British captain loudly commanded, “Let us board, or we will commence firing.”

“My men have smallpox!” Nate shouted, pointing to the flag of distress flying from the stern.

Suspicious of a trick, the "Falcon" officer decided to investigate. He noted the crew was missing on the schooner's deck, and observed the weekly wash, which was stretched over the bow to dry. Then he became concerned about an epidemic. "Where are you bound?" he asked.

"I'm going to North Carolina," Nate replied in a hoarse voice.

"You will follow closely behind my ship," ordered the "Falcon" captain. "I will fly a special flag to show that you are under my escort," he finished.

"Aye, sir," Nate answered obediently.

Nate had some terrifying moments during the cruise across the James River and Chesapeake Bay to the Atlantic Ocean. He had to sail past enemy vessels patrolling the mouth of the Elizabeth River around Portsmouth and Norfolk. To his horror, a warship fired several shots that landed dangerously close to the "Liberty Rose."

After a most suspenseful voyage, Nate and his crew docked at Edenton on a cloudy afternoon in March. By now the men were completely "cured" of their smallpox. Their plan of escape had worked beautifully, and a celebration was in order. Down below in the ship's main salon, Nate poured each man a mug of ale. A round of toasts was made.

"To Crispus, who suggested we should pretend to have smallpox, and use the weekly wash as a cover for the row of thirteen stars on the bow," Nate toasted.

From a nearby bunk, Benjamin said in a weak voice," To the best captain, who can navigate through a British blockade, with the help of the enemy."

"Here, here," shouted all, clinking their mugs together, and laughing until tears ran down their cheeks. Benjamin smiled.

"Thank you," replied Nate.

“Together, we did our best to get back home safely. The “Falcon” was truly our guardian angel,” Nate said, in good-natured playfulness.

“Here, here,” echoed the crew, downing their ale to the last drop.

After giving instructions to everyone on board his ship, Nate disembarked, and walked the few blocks to his loving family at home on W. Eden Street.

Chapter 14 - A Safer Place

"Papa, Papa!" shouted five-and-a-half-year-old Caroline, as she raced across the yard to meet her father at the gate. The adorable brown-haired child was dressed in a pink linen gown and a mobcap.

"How I've missed my pretty Caroline!" Nate exclaimed, scooping her up in his arms. He kissed Caroline on the cheek, and asked, "Where are your mama and Libby?"

"Mama is inside changing Libby's gown. Libby played in the mud," Caroline reported, as Nate lovingly carried her up the porch steps and to the front door.

Eliza was greatly relieved to have Nate safely back home. Over afternoon tea, the couple had lots of news to exchange. Pouring Nate a cup of fragrant mint tea, Eliza shared, "I've been hearing frightening rumors. Lord Cornwallis is reportedly sending forces to burn Edenton to the ground. He seems to think our people are rebellious toward British authority." Eliza sipped the soothing tea.

"That appears to be a widespread rumor," replied Nate. "I heard the same story in Virginia," he continued. "These are dangerous times, Eliza. I need to take you and the girls to a safer place, perhaps to your father's house across the bay in Tyrrell County. We can discuss this plan again tomorrow."

"How is your mother, Nate?" asked Eliza.

"My dearest Eliza, I wish I could give you good news, but we lost Mother. She was too weak by the time I was able to find a doctor for her. She is at rest with Father now," Nate sadly explained.

"I'm so sorry, Nate," Eliza said, as she got up to hug him tenderly.

A short time later, Nate reached into the pocket of his brown linen waistcoat, and took out an ancient brass key. He unlocked his father's leather-bound trunk, all scuffed and scarred, and lifted the lid. The trunk and Nate's bags had been delivered to the house earlier by the crew.

Nate announced to Eliza, "I brought some family heirlooms. Mother wanted you to have this painted fan, a silver brooch, and the green silk shawl." He presented each treasure to Eliza. "I have tea sets for the girls too," Nate finished.

"Thank you, Nate. I'll always cherish the beautiful gifts," Eliza replied tearfully.

During breakfast the next morning, Nate asked, "My sweet Eliza, can you and the girls be packed by tomorrow afternoon? Your belongings will be picked up by the crew. Then we'll sail to your father's house the following day."

Eliza answered, "I'll try my best, Nate. How long will we stay with Father?"

Nate explained, "To be on the safe side, you should plan to be away through the summer, or until the threat of danger from Cornwallis has passed. After taking you and our daughters to Tyrrell County, I will return to Edenton. Many of our townsmen are fighting in General

Washington's Army. When the time comes to evacuate Edenton, I want to be available to help these families get safely to the nearby town of Windsor in Bertie County. The people of Windsor are offering refuge."

Nate had another helping of Johnnycakes with apple butter. "Eliza, can you bring some of these cakes on our trip tomorrow? They are delicious," Nate commented.

"That's a good suggestion, Nate. Thank you, dear."

"By the way, Eliza, last night I heard important news at Horniblow's Tavern. On the Southern front General Washington was directed by Congress to choose a successor for Horatio Gates. He was the general who suffered a big defeat at the Battle of Camden, South Carolina, in August 1780. Anyway, General Washington selected Nathaniel Greene, who took over command of our Southern Army this past December. It was Greene's recommendation to remove the cannons in Edenton, so the British would not use them, if they joined Cornwallis at the Albemarle Sound. Some forty cannons were therefore dumped into the bay for a hiding spot. What a waste!" Nate finished.

Eliza commented, "I remember Father saying that the cannons were bought by Benjamin Franklin and two other American Commissioners in Paris in 1777."

"I was at the docks," Nate continued, "when the cannons were delivered in July 1778. William Borritz, the Swiss captain who lives here, brought the cannons on his ship, the "Holy Heart of Jesus."

Eliza refilled Nate's cup with coffee. "Speaking of cannons," Nate said, "I heard an amazing story out of Pennsylvania. In November 1777, the British occupied Philadelphia, our capital city. They had some 240 warships with supplies and reinforcements anchored on the Delaware River near a fort (Fort Mifflin) in Pennsylvania on Mud Island. It was reported that at one point, the British were firing cannonballs at the rate of 1,000 every 20 minutes! Incredibly, the 300 brave Continentals at the fort held off the British for almost six weeks. This heroic action allowed George

Washington the time to move his army safely to Valley Forge for winter encampment," Nate explained.

"What a story of courage. Thank you for sharing it with me," Eliza said.

On the following afternoon, several crew members arrived at Eliza and Nate's house. The men loaded two trunks of clothing and a valuable mahogany chest of drawers onto three large two-wheeled carts. The crew pushed the carts the three blocks to Nate's ship, the "Lady Albemarle."

The waterfront was a busy place that breezy April day when Nate and his family arrived at the wharves. Men shouted orders from the tall ships, and workboats bobbed at anchor. Gulls wheeled overhead with high-pitched cries. Two stray dogs barked at the commotion caused by the various animals in tow.

"Baa, baa, baa," bleated three fat sheep. Hens clucked in wooden crates, and a pig snuffled. A man and woman were herding the animals onto a periauger, that was tied up near Nate's vessel.

"Look, Mama! See the sheep!" shouted four-year-old Libby, pointing.

The excited, red-haired child almost slipped off the gangplank leading to Nate's ship.

"Libby, please hold my hand," Eliza cautioned.

Just moments after boarding her father's brig, Caroline yelled over the wind, "Mama, my straw hat just blew away!"

It would be a long sail for Eliza and the girls. Standing at the rail, they watched the town of Edenton gradually disappear, as the "Lady Albemarle" got under way in Edenton Bay. The ship was sailing east on the Albemarle Sound, and heading toward Tyrrell County.

All was not well, however, when the "Lady Albemarle" tied up at James Anderson's landing later that night. Carrying a ship's lantern, Nate led Caroline, Eliza, and Libby, up the path to the porch of the large, two-story house. One of the crew brought up the rear with another lantern.

Nate knocked loudly on the front door. Several minutes passed, and then the heavy wooden door slowly opened. James Anderson's devoted companion, Alden Cooper, stood in the doorway. Alden was wearing a blue robe over a long white nightshirt, a nightcap and slippers. He carried a tall brass candlestick that held a brightly lit candle.

Recognizing Eliza and her family, Alden said, "Good evening. Please come inside." He led the guests into the spacious passage.

Eliza explained, "Please forgive us for arriving at such a late hour, Alden. We came here for safety, as we've heard that Cornwallis is sending forces to burn Edenton to the ground. By the way, how is Father?"

Alden exclaimed, "God help us! The British Army is getting closer all the time! Your father is down with another dreadful bout of pleurisy. He is sleeping fitfully."

Yawning, Eliza added, "I'll do what I can to help, Father. The girls and I will be here for most of the summer."

"You must be tired. Let me show you to a room upstairs," Alden suggested.

Nate awoke by dawn. He left James's house and walked to the landing by the Albemarle Sound. After boarding his ship, he announced to the crew," Please transfer Eliza's two trunks and the chest of drawers to the passage of her Father's house. I'll serve a hearty breakfast upon your return."

In less than three hours, Nate and his crew were sailing west on the "Lady Albemarle" toward Edenton.

Chapter 15 - Evacuation of Edenton

Several months passed. Nate stayed in Edenton to attend to business, while Eliza and the girls had a long visit with her father in Tyrrell County. There were a few close calls that spring in Edenton when the British stole a schooner.

On a morning in mid-July, a state of chaos seemed to exist in Edenton. Alarms sounded, bells rang, and many people were rushing to an impromptu meeting on the Courthouse Green.

"Cornwallis is sending forces! The British are coming!" was the frightening message passed back and forth between the concerned citizens.

Nate spoke to the assembled crowd. "I have two ships, the "Lady Albemarle" and the "Liberty Rose." My crew and I can take up to five people, plus a few household goods and animals, per ship. Meet me at the docks and we'll take you to Windsor at no charge. The people of Windsor are offering us a safe place to stay," Nate finished.

During the remainder of the day and into the night, Nate and his crew ferried Edenton residents across the Chowan River and up the Cashie River into the town of Windsor. A few other available men helped with the evacuation, too.

There were hardly any humans, animals, or household possessions in Edenton for a week or more. Finally, good news reached Windsor! Cornwallis wasn't coming to destroy Edenton after all! Ironically, Cornwallis had problems of his own and had to change his plans.

Nate and his crew returned to Windsor. They picked up many of the weary but grateful residents of Edenton, and took them home.

Then Nate happily sailed the "Lady Albemarle" east to Tyrrell County to pick up Eliza and the girls at her father's house, and take them back home to Edenton. Nate had been separated from his family for much of 1781. How good it would be to celebrate Libby's fifth birthday in August, he thought.

Chapter 16 - News of the Battle of Guilford Courthouse

Back home in Edenton, Eliza had a special birthday surprise for Libby. Eliza invited Libby and Caroline to visit the colorful herb garden outside the kitchen. The girls would also help Eliza prepare supper that night.

In the garden, Libby picked several sprigs of mint, and put them in a basket.

"Let's gather blueberries, too." Eliza said.

"Mama, I like these tall red flowers!" Caroline exclaimed. Suddenly, while sniffing the lemon-scented red blossoms of the bee-balm, Caroline was stung on the hand by a bee. "It hurts!" she cried.

"Oh, Caroline," Eliza said, gently, kissing her daughter's injured hand. "Here, I'll crush some of these lovage leaves, and rub them on the bite to ease the pain," Eliza added.

Later that morning, a letter for Nate was delivered to the house by a messenger. Nate and the crew had gone for a sail on the Albemarle Sound. The men were checking both of Nate's ships for possible damage from the strong winds of a recent storm.

Nate arrived home that evening in time for a special birthday supper. The meal consisted of a chef salad called Salmagundi, fresh blueberries, corn muffins, tea cakes, and mint tea. A bouquet of flowers from the garden served as a cheerful centerpiece on the table.

"Happy Birthday, my dear Libby. I don't think I've had a tastier meal," Nate said. He smiled at his lovely daughters.

Both girls giggled, and then chorused, "Thank you, Papa."

As Nate sipped a second cup of tea, Eliza said, "Oh, I almost forgot, Nate. A messenger brought a letter for you this morning." Eliza sent the girls upstairs to get ready for bed. Then she handed the letter to Nate.

Puzzled, Nate commented, "I don't recall anyone who lives in Hillsborough, which is the return address on the envelope." Nate broke the red wax seal and quickly scanned the two neatly folded sheets of parchment. Suddenly, he gasped, "Oh, my God," and was deeply overcome with sorrow.

Eliza rushed to Nate's side, and put her arms around him. Concerned, she asked, "Dearest Nate, what happened?"

Between sobs, Nate sadly explained, "My brother Jessie died on March 15th during the Battle of Guilford Courthouse. This letter is from my Virginia friend, Colin Reed, who is recovering from a serious injury from that same battle."

"Oh, Nate, I'm so very sorry," Eliza said gently. She kissed Nate on the cheek and held him as her eyes filled with tears. In a moment of reflection, Eliza stated, "This has been a sad year for our family. First, your mother died, and now Jesse. I met Jesse when he was only eleven years old. I remember that he liked to observe the plants and animals in the woods."

Nate replied, "Jesse brought a lot of joy to us, particularly to Mother, after Father died. I'm glad Mother was spared the news of Jesse's death. He died a few weeks before his 18th birthday. Here is Colin's letter, if you'd like to read it, my sweet Eliza," Nate finished.

"Hillsborough, North Carolina
May 1781

Dear Nate,

You have been in my thoughts. On March 15th my thigh bone was deeply punctured by a bayonet during the Battle of Guilford Courthouse. The Quakers at New Garden nursed me for a week or so, and then I was moved by wagon to Hillsborough. My recovery is slow and painful. Ironically, I'm on King Street at the Yellow House. This is one of the taverns where Cornwallis stayed before the battle!

Nate, I truly regret if I'm the bearer of bad news, but I was saddened to learn of Jesse's death on the battlefield. Please convey my deepest condolences to your family. I've heard that Brig. Gen. Edward Stevens's brigade of

Virginians, including Jesse, fiercely fought the 71st Highlanders under Gen. Alexander Leslie. They were on the second line of fighting, which took place in the forest.

Maj. Gen. Nathaniel Greene had divided his army into three lines. The North Carolina militia was on the first line. I rode with Col. William Washington's cavalry and Thomas Watkin's company of dragoons from Virginia. We charged into the rear of the British Guards on the third line of fighting.

Even though Cornwallis won the battle, the British losses were high, especially among the officers.

For protection from the British, my wife Susannah temporarily moved from Jamestown to her parents' house in western Virginia.

Please write, Nate. If this war ever ends, I hope we can see each other again. Perhaps we can meet in Williamsburg, as we did this past February.

I send my best to you and your family for safety and good health.

Your Most Obedient Servt.

Colin Reed"

Eliza commented, "Nate, I'm glad Colin wrote to you, even though the news about Jesse broke our hearts. Let's pray that Colin recovers from his injury as soon as possible."

"Thank you for your caring words, my dear Eliza."

Chapter 17 - A Big Hope

Summer ended, and the crisp days of autumn returned. Caroline's sixth birthday was celebrated in early October. Nate sent a reply to Colin, He also wrote to Martha about Jesse's death. After the war, Nate hoped to give Jesse a proper burial at Green Ridge.

Meanwhile, Eliza was busy planning a special party for her daughters. It was a family tradition each year to commemorate the Edenton Tea Party of October 25, 1774. Eliza was one of the fifty-one ladies who bravely signed the historic resolution that was sent to London.

Libby asked, "Mama, can we use the tea sets that Papa brought us from our grandmother in Virginia?"

"That's a wonderful idea, Libby," Eliza replied. "We can also use the white teapot, sugar bowl, and creamer that belonged to my mother," Eliza added.

On the appointed day, Eliza, Caroline and Libby sat at the dining table. Eliza told her daughters the story of how she and the other courageous women signed a resolution to protest against the tax on tea.

Then Eliza poured the raspberry tea into three teacups, and handed each child a cup before making the patriotic toast. Following their mother's example, the two girls raised their teacups as Eliza proudly said, "To the pursuit of liberty from English rule."

As instructed, her daughters responded, "Here, here."

Caroline took a few sips of tea, and asked, "Mama, what does liberty mean?"

Eliza explained, "Liberty is freedom of thought and action. It is associated with being independent from another country."

Libby added, "Liberty is also my name, Caroline."

Eliza offered the girls tea cakes with the tea. She told them, "We have been at war with Britain for over six years. Maybe one day both of you will be able to tell your children how we won our independence and liberty from Britain, and started a new country. I certainly hope so," Eliza finished, as she smiled lovingly at her dear daughters.

Epilogue

Less than a week before the seventh anniversary of the Edenton Tea Party on October 25, 1774, the British surrendered at the tiny hamlet of Yorktown in Virginia. Trapped and outnumbered by the combined American-French forces, Lord Cornwallis was compelled to surrender his entire British force to General George Washington on October 19, 1781. Under the terms of surrender, the British officers were allowed to leave the former thirteen colonies. Most of the Tories, the settlers who were sympathetic to the British, went back to England or settled in British Canada.

For well over a year after the surrender, serious problems continued on the frontiers and on the high seas. On September 3, 1783, the Treaty of Paris was signed between the Americans and British, along with participation by delegates from France and Spain. This agreement brought peace, and officially formed the United States of America. The Continental Congress was granted the power to wage war and make treaties through the Articles of

Conferderation, which was ratified by every state in 1781.

In 1787, however, the Constitution, a bolder plan for the U.S. government, was framed and adopted. The Constitution is still working today!

Glossary

1. abscess: swollen, inflamed area, in the body tissue, in which pus forms

2. association: organized group of people with a common purpose

3. bayonet: large knife that can be attached to a rifle and used for stabbing or slashing in hand-to-hand fighting

4. blockade: shutting off the part of a region by ships of the enemy

5. bodice: upper part of a gown

6. brig: two-masted ship with square-rigger sails

7. brigade: army unit composed of two or more regiments

8. cannon: on land, a large mounted firearm; on sea, a gun

9. capital: official seat of government

10. cavalry: combat troops mounted on horses

11. chantey: sailor’s song

12. colonies: lands that belong to another country

13. colonists: people who live in a colony

14. commercial: business

15. condolences: expression of sympathy to another in grief

16. congress: law-making body of United States

17. conservatives: ones who oppose change

18. constitution: a plan for the government

19. counties: political divisions within a state

20. crew: those who operate a ship

21. cupola: dome

22. currency: money

23. defied: resisted

24. delegate: one who represents a group of people

25. document: official paper

26. dragoon: armed soldier capable of fighting on horseback or on foot

27. dram: one-eighth of an ounce

28. epidemic: serious outbreak of diseases, such as smallpox, typhoid, dysentery, etc.

29. estate: extensive piece of land, including a house

30. evacuation: to remove citizens from a place for protection elsewhere

31. fishmonger: one who deals in fish

32. freeholder: male who owned land

33. hall: dining room

34. heirloom: treasured possession handed down from generation to generation

35. helm: wheel

36. hull: body of a ship

37. immigrants: people who move to another country

38. independence: freedom from the control of others

39. lancet: small, surgical knife

40. liberty: freedom of thought and action

41. “liberty tea”: herbal tea

42. Loyalists: colonists in favor of king

43. mast: tall pole used to support the sails of a ship

44. merchants: those who buy and sell goods

45. militia: army composed of able-bodied men, ages 16-60, in each colony or state

46. minuteman: volunteer militiaman ready to fight at a minute's notice

47. mobcap: soft cap made of white linen or cotton and usually worn indoors

48. naval stores: tar, pitch, and turpentine used in building and maintaining ships
49. overskirt: skirt worn over a petticoat

50. parchment: skin of sheep or goat prepared as a surface on which to write

51. Parliament: law-making body of Great Britain

52. passage: hallway

53. patriotism: love and support of one's country

54. Patriots: colonists opposed to King and in favor of independence

55. periauger: two-masted workboat of colonial North Carolina

56. petticoat: bottom part of a gown

57. pleurisy: sharp, chest pain caused by inflammation of the membrane that covers a lung

58. politicians: those who hold public office

59. potpourri: mixture of dried herbs, etc.

60. powder magazine: place where gunpowder is stored

61. privateer: privately owned ship that has government permission to attack enemy ships

62. protest: strong expression of disapproval

63. provisions: food and other supplies

64. puncheon: large cask that holds from 70 to 120 gallons

65. quill pen: a pen made from the hollow stem of a large, stiff feather, sharpened point is dipped into an inkwell with ink

66. radicals: ones who want extreme change

67. refuge: place of safety

68. representation: right of being represented

69. resolution: formal statement of course of action

70. reticule: small handbag

71. revolution: far-reaching change; overthrow of existing form of government by those governed, usually by force

72. satiric: attack by making fun of
73. schooner: ship with two or more masts

74. scuttlebutt: rumor

75. sloop: sailboat with one mast

76. smallpox: major disease in 18th century; virus is spread from rash, coughing, sneezing or clothing

77. tax: money to support a government

78. toast: act of drinking in honor of person or thing

79. tradition: handing down of custom from one generation to another

80. traitor: person who betrays his or her country

81. treason: betrayal of one's country

82. tricorne: black or brown three-cornered cocked hat that is made of felt

83. trocar: surgical instrument inserted through the wall of a body cavity to withdraw fluid

84. usurpations: illegal seizures

Historical Sources

Baker, Thomas E. Another Such Victory. Eastern Acorn Press, 1999.

Butler, Lindley. North Carolina and the Coming of the Revolution. 1763-1776. Raleigh: North Carolina Department of Cultural Resources, Division of Archives and History, 1976.

Colonial Dames of America. Herbs, and Herb Lore of Colonial America. New York: Dover Publications, Inc. 1995.

Crittenden, Charles Christopher. The Commerce of North Carolina. 1776-1789. New Haven: Yale University Press, 1936.

Crow, Jeffrey J. J.A. Chronicle of North Carolina During the American Revolution. 1763-1789. Raleigh: NC Division of Archives and History, Department of Cultural Resources, 1975.

Daughters Of The American Revolution. Roster of Soldiers from North Carolina in the American

Revolution. Baltimore: Genealogical Publishing Co., Inc., 1988.

Davis, David E. History of Tyrrell County. Norfolk: James Christopher Printing, 1963.

Ganyard, Robert L. The Emergence of North Carolina's Revolutionary State Government. Raleigh: State Department of Archives and History, 1978.

Goldenberg, Joseph A. Shipbuilding in Colonial America. Charlottesville: The University Press of Virginia, 1976.

Hilowitz, Harv. Revolutionary War Chronology & Almanac 1754-1783. Saugerties, NY: Hope Farm Press, 1995.

Iredell, James, 1751-1799. The Papers of James Iredell / edited by Don Higginbotham. Raleigh: NC Division of Archives and History, Department of Cultural Resources, 1976.

Iredell, James, 1778-1783. The Papers of James Iredell / edited by Don Higginbotham. Raleigh:

NC Division of Archives and History, Department of Cultural Resources, 1976.

Jones, H.G. *North Carolina Illustrated 1524-1984*. Chapel Hill: UNC Press, 1983.

Kalman, Bobbie A. *A Colonial Town: Williamsburg*. New York: Crabtree Publishing Company, 1995.

Lefler, Hugh T. *History of North Carolina. Volume I*. New York: Lewis Historical Publishing Company, Inc., 1956.

Millar, John Fitzhugh. *Ships of The American Revolution*. Santa Barbara, California: Bellerophan Books, 1993.

Moore, Elizabeth Vann. *Guide Book Historic Edenton and Chowan County*. Edenton: Edenton Woman's Club, 1989.

North Carolina Division of Archives and History, *Historic Halifax*. Raleigh: Division of Archives and History, Department of Cultural Resources, 1976.

Olson, Sherry H. Baltimore. Baltimore: The Johns Hopkins University Press, 1980.

Parramore, Thomas C. Cradle of the Colony. Edenton: Edenton Chamber of Commerce, 1967.

Powell, William S. North Carolina Through Four Centuries. Chapel Hill: UNC Press, 1989.

Rankin, Hugh F. The North Carolina Continental Line in the American Revolution. Raleigh: State Department of Archives and History, 1977.

Robertson, J.H. Block the Chesapeake. Chesapeake: BIM-GUS Publishers, 1997.

Saunders, William L. The Colonial Records of North Carolina. Volumes IX & X. Wilmington: Broadfoot Publishing Company, 1993.

Syrett, David. The Royal Navy in American Waters. 1775-1783. Brookfield, Vermont: Scholar Press, 1989.

The Colonial Williamsburg Foundation. The Williamsburg Cookbook, China, 1975.

Tunis, Edwin. Colonial Craftsmen. New York: World Publishing Company, 1965.

Wilbur, C. Keith. Revolutionary Medicine 1700-1800. Old Saybrook, Connecticut: The Globe Pequot Press, 1997.

Wilbur, C. Keith. The Revolutionary Soldier 1775-1783. Guilford, Connecticut: The Globe Pequot Press, 1993.

Wood, Gordon S. The American Revolution: A History. New York: Modern Library, 2003.

Yolen, Jane. Sing Noel. Honesdale, PA: Boyds Mills Press, 1996.

Young, Joanne. Spirit Up The People. Birmingham: Oxmoor House, Inc., 1975.

Acknowledgments

This book would not have been possible without the information and support provided by family, organizations, and friends. A HUGE thank you goes to Faris Barbee, family historian, who shared the amazing story about our ancestor, Elizabeth Green. She was one of the fifty-one courageous women at the Edenton Tea Party, and inspired the writing of this book.

Also, the members of the Rand's Mill Chapter of the North Carolina Daughters of the American Revolution were very supportive. In particular, Regent Lynne White Belvin encouraged us to finish our original children's book on the Edenton Tea Party, as quickly as possible. Published in 1997, this book has been used as a supplementary source on early North Carolina history. We wrote two sequels to complete our children's books on the American Revolution. Over the years, we have presented numerous programs on historic Edenton to DAR chapters, libraries, schools, museums, and civic groups throughout North Carolina and beyond.

To celebrate the 250th Anniversary (July 4, 1776 to July 4, 2026) of Independence Day in the United States, Treasurer Connie Otto Barton of the Rand's Mill Chapter NSDAR, suggested a new project to us. She strongly encouraged us to combine all three of our children's books into one adult book about the American Revolution. We are grateful to Connie for her challenging idea. Our heartwarming story portrays the colonists on a personal level during the war for independence and liberty.

Additional thanks are given to the following groups and individuals: Foy and Elizabeth Barbee, Vincent and Sandy Franklin Barbee, Barker House, Books-a-Million, Broadfoot's Publishing, Dr. Josephine Brown, Camden Battlefield, City Tavern, DE Historical Society, Guilford Courthouse National Military Park, Historic Halifax, Fells Point Maritime Festival, James Iredell Association, Joel Lane House Museum, Fort Mifflin, Elizabeth Vann Moore, Moore's Creek Battlefield, Mount Vernon Ladies' Association, New Castle Historical Society, North Carolina State Capitol, North Carolina Museum of History, North Carolina Department of Public Instruction, North Carolina

Public Schools, Quail Ridge Books & Music, Pennsylvania State House, Politics and Prose, Sea Education Association, Tall Ships America, Alden Thompson, UNC Sea Grant, Valley Forge National Military Park, Wake County Public Libraries, Wake County Public Schools, Westover, Deana Whitman, Historic Williamsburg, Woman's Club of Raleigh.

As always, our beloved David Christopher Coxe, husband and Father, is with us, as our muse. His angel guides us when the written word is elusive.

About the Authors

Vivian Barbee Coxe earned her Bachelor of Science in Education degree from the University of Houston at Houston, Texas, and also did graduate work at NC State University in Raleigh, North Carolina. Mrs. Coxe taught over twenty years in the public schools of North Carolina, receiving numerous honors and grants, including two National Science Foundation grants, and the Mid-Atlantic Marine Educator of the Year award (NC, VA, MD, DE and DC) from the Mid-Atlantic Marine Education Association.

Her first book, Coastal Capers: A Marine Education Primer, was co-authored with Dr. Lundie Spence, of the UNC Sea Grant College Program. It has received remarkable success in the United States and Canada. Titusville Gold, an environmental mystery book, was published also.

Mrs. Coxe is a member of the Rand's Mill Chapter of the NC Daughters of the American Revolution, the National Society of the Daughters of the American Revolution, the Mount Vernon Ladies' Association, and the

Pennsylvania Academy of Science. She lives in Titusville, PA, with her son.

Robert Barbee Coxe graduated with honors from UNC-Asheville with a B.A. in Biology (Plant Systematics), an M.S. Biology (Plant Ecology) from UNC-Charlotte, and earned additional credit towards a Ph.D at West Virginia University in Forest Ecology. Robert has worked as a Research Scientist at UNC-Chapel Hill and the Biota of North America Program (BONAP) working on a plant polyclave of the North American Flora, as an ecologist with the Western Pennsylvania Conservancy, and most recently as the State Ecologist for the State of Delaware. He is also a former President of the Pennsylvania Academy of Science. Currently, Robert is an owner/web designer for Silphium Design LLC.

www.ingramcontent.com/pod-product-compliance
Lightning Source LLC
LaVergne TN
LVHW051004080826
845145LV00009B/2442

* 9 7 8 1 7 3 7 5 8 9 3 3 4 *